A Mail-Order HEART

JANELLE DANIELS

Dream Cache Publishing

Dream Cache Publishing

A MAIL-ORDER HEART

ISBN-13: 978-0692712276
ISBN-10: 0692712275

Printed in the United States of America

DEDICATION

To Kristi, Stephanie, Tracy, Amy, and Dan. You all made
this possible. Thank you

Chapter One

There came a time when a person had to admit they were insane. Clara reached that point yesterday.

Dusting off her new traveling skirt, more brown in color than gray thanks to the dirt and grime that had accumulated on the fabric over the past week and a half of travel, she stepped onto the train platform in Promise Creek.

She might be crazy for traveling so far to marry a man she'd never met, but she wanted to look good for Ivan, her mail-order groom. It was the least she could do after he'd helped her out of a bad situation. Besides, he would be her husband, and while she didn't see herself as a breathtaking beauty, she was passably pretty, and she hoped her future husband would find her rich chestnut hair and sparking blue eyes appealing, regardless of her state of dress.

She curved her cupid-bow lips at the corners, glancing around for a man equally as unsure of who he was looking for. No doubt they'd be the only two left on the platform in a few moments once the other passengers left in search of a quick lunch.

Her hand shook, but she stilled it. She would not show any nerves when her future husband first saw her. She wanted him to know that she felt confident, secure in her decision to marry him. Besides, she wasn't some timid woman who feared the future. She embraced it.

And she *would* embrace him as soon as she saw him. It was best to start things off warmly between them.

The Promise Creek Station was small compared to others they'd stopped at, but there was still a thirty-minute layover where travelers could alight and stretch their legs while the train took on new cargo and passengers.

Clara handed the porter a ticket to claim her baggage and waited until he brought her trunk to her. She wouldn't leave it in case someone decided to steal it. She didn't have much, but she refused to part with the few items she'd brought from home to remember her parents and siblings by.

Ivan would have to come to her.

As the minutes passed, Clara's shoulders slouched, and she went from perfect posture, to leaning against her trunk, to finally, using it as a seat.

Where was Ivan? Had he changed his mind or forgotten her?

Of course not. She was his bride. No man would forget to pick up his bride, would he? And there was no reason he'd change his mind. In his letters, he'd expressed how much he wanted her to come.

But she didn't know the man well. She'd only received two letters from him before her mother urged her to accept his proposal. In a family with twelve children, she the eldest, and not enough food to feed them all, her choices had been limited to two—take a position as a factory worker, knowing her life would be shortened from the strenuous labor, or take her chances out west as a mail-order bride since no men in town had chosen to make her their wife.

After her mother's urging, she'd chosen marriage.

But oh, how she missed the babies back home. Her twin sisters, the youngest of the brood, used to climb into her bed as she told them stories that filled their little two-year-old minds with wonder.

She bit her lip, swallowing the lump forming in her throat. She would not cry here. She'd held it together the entire trip, and she would *not* break down moments before she met her future husband.

The train whistled as the locomotive pulled from the deserted station. Large tufts of smoke shot from the engine, and she could almost taste the sooty granules on her tongue.

Sweat slicked her neck at its departure.

What would she do if he didn't come for her? She'd have to make arrangements for lodging that night. Mentally counting what was left in her purse, she hesitated spending any of it until she knew how long she'd need to make it last. One night in an upper-crust hotel would take half of what she possessed.

"Is there someone you're waiting for, ma'am?"

An elderly gentleman asked, clutching a faded grey cap in his hands.

Relief pumped through her. She wasn't completely alone now. "Yes. I'm waiting for my fiancé."

The man gulped, wringing his hat. "You're here for Crazy Ivan, aren't you?"

"Crazy Ivan?" *Heavens.* "I don't think we're thinking of the same man. I'm Ivan Pavlova's fiancée."

The man winced. "I was afraid you'd say that. Come on. I'll bring you to the others."

"What others?"

He glanced over his shoulder. "The other women here to marry Crazy Ivan."

Her feet rooted to the platform. "I beg your pardon?" Surely she hadn't heard him correctly. There couldn't be anyone else there to marry Mr. Pavlova. She was his fiancée and had letters to prove it. There had to be some other explanation. The man she'd corresponded with wouldn't just throw her over without writing to her.

"You're the ninth woman claiming to be Ivan's mail-order bride today."

"The ninth?" she screeched. This couldn't be happening. She'd traveled too far, given up too much. "Where is Ivan? Is he with the other women?" Ivan had to straighten this out. She was out of money, and going home wasn't possible. Her family had barely scraped by, and only because her mother sacrificed two of her three meals a day.

Clara had to marry Ivan Pavlova. Today. There was no other option.

The man's shoulders slumped. "Perhaps you should join the group, and let them explain."

Oh, no. He wasn't getting away without giving her more information. "Sir, I must insist that you tell me where my fiancé is immediately. He can clear up this misunderstanding. I'm not moving from this spot until you tell me what I want to know."

He sighed and turned back toward her with pity in his eyes. "He's dead, ma'am. Crazy Ivan died three days ago."

WHEN A NINTH BRIDE WALKED into the hotel lobby, Sheriff Sawyer Morrison was ready for murder. *Damn it, Ivan.*

As that thought came, Sawyer shook it right out. That was no way to think about the dead. However, if Ivan wasn't dead already, Sawyer was willing to bet one of the women screeching in the cleared-out lobby would happily perform the task.

"Oh, no!" A dark-haired girl, the loudest of the bunch, hollered once she spotted the newcomer. "No. No. Ivan was *my* fiancé!"

Sawyer snaked an arm around the banshee before she could sink her claws into the pretty brunette with the widest brown eyes he'd ever seen. "Now, Miss…" What *was* her name? She'd yelled it enough times he should remember, but honestly, he'd blocked every word shrieked from her mouth. "We'll get this sorted out in no time. Restrain yourself. I won't ask again. If you attack one more person, I'll be forced to put you in a cage. Neither of us wants that."

He sure didn't. In a town bursting with single, wealthy men ready to establish families after their mines paid out—and too few women—he'd get an earful for throwing a woman in jail. Good reason or no.

When she stopped fighting him, he released her slowly and turned his attention to the newcomer.

How would she react to the news? Not only about Ivan's death, but about the other women. From what he'd seen from the others, she'd either scream in anger like Banshee or she'd melt into a puddle of tears.

He eyed the sturdy traveling dress and guessed the latter. A woman used to work, as her dress suggested, wouldn't have time for a tantrum. But even as he thought of her possible reactions, the attractive curves showcased by the plain garment distracted him.

He was a man. His visceral reaction wasn't anything he was ashamed of, but it was damned inconvenient. Not to mention, wrong. This woman had come to marry another man.

But that man was dead.

He cleared his throat, steering his thoughts into a more appropriate line of thought as he doffed his hat and approached her. "I'm Sheriff Morrison, ma'am. Am I correct to assume that you're Ivan Pavlova's fiancée?"

She nodded once, her eyes wide as she glanced at the group of women behind him.

He stepped in her line of sight, and her gaze

jerked to his. Clashing. Holding. Melding.

The power of those coffee-bean eyes robbed him of breath.

Mercy. She was divine.

"Are those women also claiming to be fiancées?" she asked, but didn't try to peek at the madness behind him.

So, she already knew.

He looked to the old porter, and the man shrugged. "She made me tell."

Sawyer raised a brow before turning his attention back to the woman. It wasn't hard to loosen the man's lips. "You're aware that you're the ninth woman claiming to be engaged to Ivan Pavlova's, and that he passed three days ago?" he asked, making sure she had received correct information.

"Yes. I am aware of the facts."

Sawyer leaned forward, ready to catch her mid-swoon if need be.

Please don't faint.

His wish came true. She didn't pass out. She didn't cry or scream either.

Her face impassive, she didn't move a muscle. She didn't clench her fists, didn't yell. Didn't even blink. Blank eyes stared into his, lost. Alone.

Numb.

She'd gone completely numb.

Damn.

He'd seen enough shock to know the signs. Joining a lawless gold rush town at its peak did that. He'd witnessed more thefts and murders than he cared to think about. The victims lucky enough to survive such ordeals bore the same look plastered on this woman's face.

"What's your name, ma'am?" he whispered, worried he'd spook her.

After a moment, deadened eyes trailed up from his chest. "Clara… Clara Stewart."

He nodded slowly, allowing her time to get used to the new circumstances.

With a deep breath, her eyes lost some of the lifelessness and she lifted her chin. "What will happen now? I can't go home."

Before he could speak, the other women shouted again.

Banshee yelled, "I can't go home either!"

"If anyone gets to stay, it'll be me," a blond woman asserted.

Another one cried.

He closed his eyes, lifting his face toward the ceiling. Lord, help him.

When the women jostled each other, he stepped forward. "Don't make me follow through with my threat." All the women froze at his words.

Good. At least he had some power over the situation. "I know you're all worried and scared. It's understandable. But I promise you, we'll get this all straightened out. There's no need to panic. None of you will be sent home. I summoned the mayor, and he'll figure out a solution that is acceptable to you all. Until he arrives, I need you to remain calm even if twenty more brides walk into this room."

He lost them at that point. With the idea of twenty more women claiming to be the fiancée of the half-crazed miner, the group went berserk.

"But how will I find a husband if there's almost

thirty brides?" one of them wailed.

Two others madly faced off while another outright screamed. Sawyer was ready to throw his hands in the air and walk away. Or better yet, he'd lock them in the jail and let them fight it out amongst themselves. "Look—"

Clara stepped forward. "Everyone, calm down." Her words were quiet but firm.

Sawyer's jaw sagged when the volume in the room dropped immediately. His head snapped toward the soft-spoken miracle worker and wanted to kiss her feet.

She stepped closer to the group. "We need to think right now. This is horrible. Absolutely horrible. We all needed a marriage to Ivan or we wouldn't be here. I've traveled hundreds of miles, and I know you've all come just as far."

Several of the women nodded, although Banshee's lips pressed together, her arms folding with a huff.

Clara rewarded the group with a small, reassuring smile. "I'm sure the mayor will be able to do something for us. We're women who've come to Promise Creek in good faith. Surely, the town will help us in some way. Isn't that right, Sheriff?"

He jumped at the chance to help her. "Yes. Everything will be taken care of."

The bright smile she gave him made him feel ridiculously pleased. One smile shouldn't have impacted him that much.

"See? You've heard it from the sheriff himself. Everything will work out."

Chapter Two

Clara's heart fluttered when an appreciative smile crossed the sheriff's lips. She could tell he'd been two seconds away from losing his temper at the bunch of raging women, and Clara had no desire to see such a sight.

Not that a blow up wasn't deserved.

The women were crazy. Did they not realize that each and every one of them felt the same about the situation? Each woman was upset. Desperate. Clara wanted to lay down and throw a tantrum of epic proportions, but who would that help? Certainly not herself. And certainly not everyone else in the group.

It was time to be calm, logical. There had to be a solution to this mess.

She stepped forward and joined the group of women, several of them trying to talk over the others.

"Thank you for what you did," a woman with light brown hair said, a grateful grin lighting her face. "I thought they were going to brawl like those men you hear about in saloons over a..."—her cheeks flushed with color—"woman of ill repute."

Clara smiled broadly, hoping to put the woman at ease. "Well, we couldn't have that. I'm Clara Stewart."

"Isabelle Sweeney. Just call me Belle though, most people do."

"All right, Belle."

A portly gentleman entered the room then, his hands held high once the group of women screeched at his arrival. "Ladies, please. Please!"

Clara stepped forward, turning her back on the gentleman to face the women. "Let's hear him out first. Remember, this isn't his fault. He's here to help us."

A few women put their heads down in shame, shoulders sinking as they realized how ridiculous their behavior was.

Clara nodded before turning back toward the man. "Please continue, sir."

His chin wobbled as it notched up in importance. "I am Mayor Bracken. I've been informed of the damn terrible circumstances."

One of the women squeaked at the language, and the mayor turned a questioning brow toward Sheriff Morrison.

The sheriff raised his hands like he had no idea what the woman's problem was. Clara held back her snort. But just barely.

The gray-haired man continued with the shake of

his head, "As I was saying, I know you've all come to Promise Creek in hopes of a union with Crazy—er—Ivan Pavlova. Unfortunately, that isn't possible now that he's dead. However—" he raised his voice when the women began panicking— "However, there are still possibilities for marriages if that's what you're after."

A petite blonde whispered, "Marriages? But I thought Ivan was dead."

Clara cleared her throat. "What marriages are you speaking of? Other men in town, I presume?"

"Exactly."

"I can't just marry anyone!" the blonde cried.

Another huffed. "I came to marry a wealthy man."

The murmuring collided then as each and every woman said her piece about the news.

Clara tried to calm them, but had no luck this time. Instead, she turned her attention to the mayor. "Sir, I think I speak for the rest of us when I say that we aren't comfortable marrying just anyone. We've all corresponded with Ivan," she said, only guessing that each woman had exchanged letters with the scoundrel, "and we took a chance on him because we felt we knew him."

Belle nodded her agreement, moving to stand beside her. "I traded several letters with Ivan before I felt comfortable traveling all this way. I don't like the idea of jumping into anything permanent with someone I don't feel is a good match."

"Now, hold on, ladies." The mayor quickly held up his hands again before the women unraveled. "I'm not asking you to march up to the church with a groom today. In fact, I'm hoping for the opposite."

Intrigued, Clara couldn't stay silent. "What do you mean?"

"What I mean is, if you nine women are willing to stay in Promise Creek, the men of this town would like to fulfill one of Ivan's promises." The women were silent for once. "We've decided that if you *all* agree to stay, Ivan's house and his mine will legally be turned over to you."

Belle gasped, but Clara waited for the catch. No one gave anything away without expecting something in return.

The vicious brunette who tried to claw her eyes out earlier had obviously come to the same conclusion when she asked, "And why would the town be willing to give us such a valuable gift?"

"Well, you're new so I'm sure you haven't noticed, but we're short on women. You've come here to be mail-order brides, and it's our hope that you'll stay, live in Ivan's extensive house, work the mine or hire workers, and allow our men to court you."

Several of the women clapped and cheered.

"That is most generous of you, Mayor Bracken." Clara nodded her thanks. "Would you allow us a few moments to discuss your offer?"

"Of course. But I would like to stress that it's an all or nothing deal. If one of you decides to return home, the other eight don't get the house or mine. Other arrangements will of course be made to make sure you all get home safely, or you may choose to enter a union immediately."

Clara swallowed hard, but nodded. They all had

to agree. This group of nine, emotional women, had to come to a consensus in the next five minutes.

Lord, help her.

Sheriff Morrison gestured for the mayor to head out of the building. "Let's give them some privacy while they discuss their options.

When the men headed out, the noise level increased as each woman spoke louder, hoping their words would be heard.

"I say we stay."

"This is our chance."

"What if none of the men are to our liking?"

"I don't like this. Something seems off."

Clara held up her hands for silence.

When eight sets of eyes locked onto hers, she lowered her hands. "I know this is a lot to take in. We were expecting one thing, handed another, and now we've been given this option. I'm here because I had no other choice. It was either take a mail-order bride position or go work in a factory. I chose the former. I didn't envision this for my life, and I'm guessing none of you did either."

She waited until each woman nodded.

"Now, we have a big decision to make. It's all or nothing. We can all stay and live in Ivan's house. You heard the mayor. It's huge. Ivan told me in his letters that while his mine hasn't paid out, it was sure to soon. Almost all other claims in the area have struck big. That tells me two things. One, there's a possibility we could strike it rich. And two, the men in this town have already done so. They're rich. Miners who are now millionaires. That sounds like a good starting off point for the future."

When the other women nodded, she grinned. "My vote is to stay here and take my chances. This is a better arrangement than what I came for. We will be provided for, have a nice home, and we will be able to get to know gentlemen before we agree to marry them. We are needed here. We hold all the cards. I can't see a better situation for me. What about you?"

Most of the women agreed, but the dark-haired woman stood stubbornly to the side, her blue-glass eyes mutinous.

"What's your name?" Clara asked her.

"Violet Morgan."

Clara lifted her chin, but spoke kindly. Violet was not going to intimidate her. "Is there something you'd like to add, Violet?"

Her face expressionless, she looked over the group of women as if sizing them up. "You're all here to marry. But so am I. What if there aren't enough desirable men in town like they say? What if we're left competing with one another over one or two men? Or, what happens if one of us decides to leave after a week?"

Clara understood Violet's concern, but wished the woman wouldn't speak so harshly to the group. They weren't enemies. "Those are good questions. And we'll need to get answers before we decide on anything. But we aren't competing with one another. I'm sure if we sat down and talked for a longer period, we'd see that we're interested in very different types of men."

Violet sneered. "I think we can safely assume we're all interested in wealthy men."

The group turned miraculous shades of red.

Clara hated seeing the looks of embarrassment and shame. "That's nothing to be ashamed of," Clara soothed. "Many of us come from common backgrounds it seems. I see nothing wrong with hoping for an easier life."

Violet didn't apologize, but her shoulders lowered as if she regretted her words.

Once everyone settled down again, Clara said, "I don't want to pressure anyone into anything you don't want to do. But there are huge benefits to staying. Raise your hand if you would be willing to remain here, in Ivan's house, and take your chances with the mine and the men in town."

Clara raised her hand with another six of the women. After a moment, a freckled red-head, her body reed thin under an unfortunate gray dress raised her hand. That only left Violet.

A few women glared at her.

"We can't do this without you," Clara whispered.

"I'm not good at this whole group thing."

Belle rolled her eyes. "No kidding."

Violet stiffened at the remark. "I don't know if this is what's best for me."

"What other options do you have?" Belle asked. "If they were any good, you wouldn't be here, would you?"

Violet's lips tightened, but not before her lip trembled.

Clara felt bad for Violet, but the woman had a sharp temperament. If they ended up living together, Clara knew they'd have their hands full keeping the fighting to a minimum.

"All right. I'll stay."

The group sighed in relief, and Clara closed her eyes in gratitude. "Thank you." Turning her attention to everyone else she said, "I want you to know that we're in this together. I want you all to be happy. I'll do everything in my power to see you all happily married if it's the last thing I do. We're sisters now. From here on out, we're family. And I take care of my family."

"Here, here!" Belle cheered.

The group broke out in squeals over their good fortune, ecstatic at the turn of events. Everyone but Violet, of course.

Clara's lips curved into a tentative smile. "I guess all we have to do is tell the mayor we agree."

While Clara wanted to celebrate with the others, her eyes kept trailing back to Violet. It wouldn't be all wishes and rainbows with that one around.

Chapter Three

From the moment the women agreed to stay, Sawyer smelled trouble. Not that he didn't appreciate what they were doing. A lot of men would be happy with the situation, and it would bring even more respectability to their town as couples married and had families.

Their town needed that sort of stability. Promise Creek wouldn't stay a mining town forever.

Sawyer lightly flicked the lines as he maneuvered a wagon full of women down the road. Mayor Bracken and he had agreed that it'd be best to install the women in Ivan's house before announcing their presence to the town.

Smartest thing they could've done. Sawyer didn't relish the mess they'd have on their hands when word got out about the women.

Sawyer inhaled Clara's scent a moment before she moved up from the back of the wagon to speak with him. "How far is Ivan's ranch, Sheriff?"

Sawyer closed his eyes against his body's reaction to her voice. From the moment she'd walked into the hotel's lobby, his body went on alert. He was more aware of her than he'd ever been of any woman. He could almost smell the rose soap on her skin when she'd been across the room, practically taste the cherry softness of her plush lips or feel the sun's warmth in her glossy mahogany hair, just by glancing at her.

He didn't look at her now. Instead, he gave extra attention to the horses. The last thing he wanted to do was make a fool of himself. The women would view such spectacles in the future, but he refused to turn himself into some slobbering idiot.

Oh, he'd been fine just being the town's unattached sheriff. Hadn't given a second thought to courting women in the next town or ordering a mail-order bride of his own.

At least not until he'd set eyes on one intended for Ivan.

Now he couldn't stop thinking about it.

He cleared his throat. "The house is located twenty-minutes outside town."

"So far?"

He turned in time to catch the adorable frown on her face. "Far? His house is one of the closer ones. There are ranchers who live several hours away."

She flushed beet red, and it took all his will power not to smile at the sight.

"Pardon. I'm from New York. Most things are located within a few miles. I had no idea towns were this spread out in the West." She gazed out at the wildflower covered hills.

The earth's natural carpet still took his breath away after all this time. He and his brother had grown up on the streets of New York after their parents' murders. The filth they used to search through for scraps to eat, the hovel they slept in, rarely came back to him. They'd been lucky to make it out alive.

And now look at him.

He dragged in a deeply scented breath, the pure air charging him—

A gun shot rang from behind them.

A few of the girls screamed as the wagon lunged forward.

He swore, pulling the lines, struggling to keep the animals under control. Hooves thundered down the road behind them, several sets, and Sawyer knew he only had a moment to bring the wagon to a stop.

"Yeehaw! What'd I tell ya, Simon? I told ya I'd heard there was women!"

The three loathsome miners who approached were the last people Sawyer hoped to see. They were more drunks and town troublemakers than miners after their claims ran dry. Their main purpose, as far as Sawyer could tell, was to cause problems for the people who'd struck it rich.

"You were right, Horace. Never thought old Jimmy might be tellin' the truth. But woo-ee—" he whistled through his teeth as he eyed Clara "—was he not lyin'. That one there is mine," he said, claiming her as his own.

Over my dead body.

Sawyer was ready to rip Simon's eyes from his

head, but the horses shied, and he gave his full focus to them. Maiming the men would have to wait. "Whoa. Steady. Easy now." With a final snort, one horse settled down, calming the rest. "Good. That's good."

When Sawyer was sure the wagon was safe from spooked horses, he casually turned toward the men. Coming on too aggressive would only provoke them. "I don't know what you heard, but these women aren't up for grabs."

"Whatcha mean?" Simon scratched his butt in the saddle. "These aren't them mail-order brides Crazy Ivan went and bought?"

Banshee sneered. "No one bought me. No one ever will."

Sawyer lifted his face toward the sky. *Save me*, he pleaded before turning his attention back on the men who looked like they'd swallowed lemons. "Listen, fellas." He turned on whatever charm he could muster. "This will all be sorted out soon. Mayor Bracken set a meeting tonight at the church to explain everything. Until then, you need to return to town, and let me do my job."

Horace spit. "I think you should do some explainin' now, Sheriff."

When Simon eyed Clara again, Sawyers fingers twitched near his colt. "I told you as much as you need to know. Now, I'm not going to ask again. Head back to town."

Simon's eyes slid between his cohorts before he went for his gun.

The women gasped when Sawyer had his gun out and pointed at Simon's heart before the bedraggled miner cleared his weapon.

The three held up their hands.

Horace shook his head. "No need for that, Sawyer. We'll wait to hear what the mayor has to say. Isn't that right, Simon?" He looked at his companion, but the man only glared.

Sawyer didn't move. His gun never wavered as he stared at the man's eyes, waiting. Watching. Looking for a flicker in the deadened depths.

The man was bad news. When Simon's mine hadn't paid out, he'd drowned his sorrows in the bottom of a bottle. He'd never crawled out.

Simon sneered, finally relaxing his hands away from his gun. "Sure thing, Horace. Let's see what Mayor Do-Gooder has to say about this." His eyes narrowed on Sawyer. "Just keep your paws off the merchandise, Morrison."

Banshee rose from the wagon. "Why you—"

Fortunately, Clara reached out to Banshee before she could do anything else.

The three men rode away, but not before Simon raked another lurid glance over Clara.

Anger boiled Sawyer's blood, but he swallowed it, holstering his gun with sharp control. "Are you all okay?

The women nodded except Banshee. She pressed her lips together before looking away.

"We'll all be fine," Clara whispered. "Let's just get to the house."

Sawyer nodded. They would be fine because he'd be leaving them his shotgun.

He couldn't get them safely locked behind doors soon enough to please him.

WHEN THE MEN RODE AWAY, Clara held her body ramrod straight, her chin lifted high. It was the only way she knew how to deal with the terror choking her.

Even now, after such a short amount of time, the group of women looked to her for how to react. And she wouldn't let them down.

She sat calmly, her hands folded in her lap. If her knuckles were a little whiter than normal, she hoped no one else noticed. She needed to look composed, carefree. Even if she was screaming inside.

"Can we really do this?" Belle whispered to her. "You saw those men back there. What if they're all like that?"

"They're not." Clara looked off in the distance, breathing deeply of the flowered hills. "The sheriff and mayor appear to be gentlemen. I assume that's what most of the men are like."

"And if they're not?"

"Then we'll figure out how to handle it."

Clara meant exactly what she said. They would stay as long as it was the right thing for them. No one would force any of them into anything they didn't want to do. They weren't slaves. And they certainly hadn't been bought no matter what the men had said.

When they rounded a bend in the road, a towering two-story structure came into view. The wrap around porch held a swing suspended from the ceiling, and pots overflowed with a kaleidoscope of color. The pitched roofline gave it a whimsical appearance, and the large, paned windows sparkled.

Sheriff Morrison slowed the horses. "This is it. Ivan's house—your house now."

One of the girls squealed.

Clara couldn't blame her. Her mouth gaped open at the sheer size of the wooden structure. "This is ours?" She glanced at the handsome man who'd taken the time to escort them.

"Yes. Were you expecting something else?"

"Honestly? Smaller." The mayor had called it extensive, but that word varied in definition. She was sure there were grander houses, but this structure wasn't anything to sneeze at.

He grinned. "I hope it doesn't disappoint." He leaped to the ground and rounded the wagon before holding up his arms to help her down.

"Of course not." She placed her hands on his shoulders without thinking, but the minute her fingers felt the muscles beneath his shirt, her body jerked with awareness. She could feel the heat of his skin, the cords of rippling muscle, and that power shot a thrill through her.

His hands encircled her waist, and he lifted her down quickly, releasing her a little too abruptly before moving on to help the next woman.

"Thank you," she said, but further words caught in her throat.

What was wrong with her? She'd been assisted from vehicles her entire life, but never had such a touch unnerved her.

And he wasn't even affected by it! He'd just gone on and helped Belle down without hesitation. This was not the way she wanted to start off her time in

Promise Creek. She may have come to marry Ivan, and even if that wasn't possible now, she still intended on marrying someone. It would do her no good to set her heart on the sheriff so soon. She couldn't think about marrying anyone until she helped the other women. They needed to come first.

If all else failed, Clara could take care of herself. By the looks of some of the other women, they couldn't say the same thing.

Sheriff Morrison led them into the house. "It's large, but we haven't gone through the house yet to know if you'll need more supplies or beds. I want you ladies to take a good look around, and let me know if there's something you need. The town will do their best to provide it. As mentioned earlier, the mine belongs to you. However, you'll need to work the claim to make money. Everything Ivan made went into building this house—and apparently ordering brides. Unless you find money hidden somewhere, you'll need to start tapping the mine. The town will, of course, help with necessities for the next few days until you're on your feet."

One of the blondes stepped closer to the sheriff. "That is very kind of you."

A frown marred Clara's forehead as the girl sweetly batted long black lashes. A flare of jealousy scorched her before she tamped it down. Getting riled over a man, especially one that wasn't hers, was pointless. They would all have to live together for the foreseeable future, and bickering over men like dogs over a bone would only make things worse.

But as the woman placed a hand on the sheriff's

arm, Clara almost said something she'd regret. Instead, she opted for, "This is more than adequate, Sheriff. Thank you so much for bringing us out here. We'll let you know if there's anything we need."

He looked around uneasy. "Are you sure you don't want me to stay until you've taken stock?"

The blonde smiled. "That would be gr—"

"Absolutely not." Clara forced a smile. "If there is anything pressing, I'll ride into town and inform you."

His eyes met hers then, and air clogged her lungs as he quietly assessed her.

Could he see the flush bruising her body? The blood rushing through her veins a little more quickly? The air heaving from her lungs? Heavens, she hoped not.

"Do you know how to saddle a horse?"

She nodded a little too hard. "Yes. We'll manage just fine."

He handed over a shotgun, and her hand wrapped around the cold metal. "I want you to have this. You shouldn't need it, but I don't feel right leaving you without it. Do you know how to use it?"

She wasn't the best shot, but she could manage if needed. Perhaps one of the others had more experience. In either case, she was grateful for it. "Well enough. Thank you."

After a final look, he placed his hat back on his head. "All right, then. I'll also leave the wagon in case you need it."

"That's very kind."

After he left, Clara's shoulders sagged. She

shouldn't let him affect her that way. It would only cause problems.

The blonde looked at her with a frown. "Why did you have him leave?"

Clara cleared her throat. "I, um, thought we needed to have some time alone to figure things out. A lot has changed, and I fear that with nine women, it'll be difficult to come to an agreement."

The girl slowly smiled. "You're probably right. I'm Olivia by the way."

"Clara." She smiled at the girl before heaving a sigh. "Come on. Let's round up the others and figure things out."

She hoped it wouldn't be as hard as she imagined.

Chapter Four

It was a nightmare.

Growing up in a house with twelve kids trained Clara how to handle volatile situations. What she wasn't prepared for was nine women, all with strong personalities, who had no ties of familial love moderating their responses.

From the moment she entered the parlor, the arguing began.

Clara walked to the center of the room. "Listen, everyone. Listen, please!" When the room quieted down, she tossed them a thankful, weary smile. "Look, I know we're all upset. But shouting at each other won't help the situation. We're in this together, and the sooner we start working with one another, the better off we'll be. We'll all get what we want. We have options, but before we discuss them, I'd like us all to introduce ourselves."

A few nodded their agreement, however reluctantly.

"Good." She sat down in a curvy chair, one no man would ever enjoy sitting in, and waited for everyone to take her cue and arrange themselves comfortably—or at least as comfortably as the stiff, formal furniture would allow. Why anyone wanted such unaccommodating chairs—with pale silk fabric no less—was beyond her. Keeping such material clean in a family environment was an effort worthy of Sisyphus. "I'll begin since I suggested it. I'm Clara Stewart. I'm from New York City and grew up in a large family. I answered Ivan's advertisement because there wasn't enough food for everyone. It was this or factory work, and I chose this path."

When she finished, she nodded encouragingly at Belle. No one seemed willing to jump in, and Clara was determined for the women to get to know one another. They would all be in each other's lives for the foreseeable future, after all.

The girl's lips quirked. "I guess that means I'm next."

The woman with the reddest hair Clara had ever seen snickered.

"I'm Isabelle Sweeney, but I go by Belle. I'm from St. Louis and recently orphaned." Her voice cracked a little at the end, and she coughed before continuing. "My parents were killed a few months ago, and I had no where else to go."

"No other family?" Olivia asked softly, her delicate hands folded primly on her lap.

"No."

A few of the girls murmured their condolences.

The other blonde stepped forward. "I'm Willow

Packer. I'm from Boston. I ran away from an arranged marriage to a man twice my age. My parents thought it was for the best, but I didn't. I refuse to let others choose my path. So I answered Ivan and decided my own fate."

The first impression Clara got was that Willow was hard. Determined. Those qualities would serve the whole group well. A woman like that would never allow another to walk over her. "Why don't you go next, Olivia?" Clara suggested.

"All right. I'm Olivia Hardy." She tucked a loose dirty-blond curl behind her ear. "I'm from Georgia. I can't say anything terrible happened to me or that I needed to come. I didn't."

The woman so fond of screeching raised a brow. "Then why on earth are you here?"

Clara frowned at the dark-haired girl, but she only shirked a cerulean silk-encased shoulder.

That one's trouble. It didn't take a genius to figure that out.

Olivia raised a hand to her neck as she gently cleared her throat. "I wish I had a good reason for being here. But the truth is, I felt sorry for him. He seemed so lonely. And I guess I was too. It's what prompted me to write him. And as he told me of his life here, I thought I might be able to bring him some comfort."

The shrewish woman picked a perfectly manicured nail. "A lot of good it did you."

"Thank you for that," Clara chastised. "Since you're already talking, why don't you go next?" Not that Clara actually wanted to know anything about her. She might have the facade of a goddess, all curves with sinfully dark hair and icy-blue eyes, but after all the screaming and sarcastic comments, she'd been a headache to deal with.

The woman smiled bitingly. "I'm Violet Morgan as some of you already know. I'm from New York. *Fifth-Avenue*," she stressed. "I came for Ivan's money."

The room went dead silent.

While Ivan's wealth no doubt played into each of the girls' decisions to marry him, Clara knew there were other reasons each and every one of them were here. "His money? If you're from Fifth-Avenue, why not stay and marry someone equally endowed?"

"It's complicated." Violet glared. "And Irrelevant."

Clara was a patient woman, and she liked to think she was kind. But there was something about Violet that got under her skin. Clara hoped that whatever had driven Violet from New York would eventually soften her. If not, Violet was bound to have a difficult life.

"Since we're all getting along so great—" the red-head looked between Clara and Violet "—why don't I go next?"

One of the girls who hadn't gone yet snorted as she leaned against the mantle. "Go on. Hopefully it will diffuse the war brewing."

Freckles scrunched on the red-head's nose as she grinned. "I'm Aria McKinnon. I'm from Philadelphia. And Irish—" she waved a hand over her flaming locks "—if that wasn't obvious. There wasn't anyone in my area willing to court me outside of the Irish community. I didn't find anyone suitable. Ivan told me he liked spirited red-heads, and being that he was the only one that had ever said that besides my father, I came to marry him."

Clara chuckled with Aria. Out of everyone, Aria had the best attitude. Hearing her speak was like a breath of fresh air after spending a hot summer's day mucking out stalls. She'd kept a cheerful temperament through the whole ordeal, and Clara was grateful for that. "I'm glad you're here."

The light brunette leaning against the fireplace stepped forward. "I'm Rosalie Davis. I'm from a small farming town in Ohio. I wanted adventure. A new life. I've heard about the Montana Territory and the miners here. It all seemed so exciting, and I wanted to be a part of it. It was either marry a miner or stake a claim myself," she teased.

Belle chuckled. "Well, it looks like you have a claim of your own now. We all do."

"True." Rosalie exhaled a satisfied breath.

The petite woman on the end of the sofa appeared more elven than human with her large dark eyes and black hair. The creamy white of her skin looked as if it hardly ever saw sunlight. "And you?" Clara asked.

"Juliette Cameron from Charleston. I came to Ivan because I had to get out of my town, and I needed a fresh start."

The room quieted again, and Clara felt sorry for her.

Juliette squirmed uncomfortably on the cushion and looked at her feet. "My brother is a bank robber on the run." Olivia gasped at the news, but Juliette continued on as if telling it all quickly would somehow be easier. "I was accused of helping him rob the bank next to a library where I often volunteered, but a jury found me innocent of all charges. I *am* innocent. However, the people in town never looked at me the same."

Clara wasn't sure she could either. Not that she condemned Juliette for her brother's actions. But seeing her, a quiet slip of a woman, Clara would've never guessed she'd been accused of grand larceny. "I'm sorry. I hope you find your fresh start."

The final woman slumped on the couch, her smooth auburn hair obscuring her face, and she flinched when all attention turned to her. "Sadie. Sadie Johnston," she said, barely speaking above a whisper. "I'm a widow from Maryland. I had no where else to go after my husband died, so I answered Ivan's advertisement."

Clara's heart pinched for the woman. Being a lone woman in the world was hard. "When did he pass?"

Sadie rubbed her stomach nervously. "A few weeks ago."

It was obviously distressing for her to talk about it, and Clara had no intention of making Sadie any more uncomfortable than she already was.

What must it be like to love someone so deeply it hurt to even speak of them? Clara sighed, wondering if she'd ever know.

"Well, all right," Clara said. "Now that we've introduced ourselves and know a little more about each other, I think it's time we made a plan for our future. At least the immediate one. The first issue we should tackle is money. What are we going to do about it?"

"That shouldn't be a problem, the town said they'd provide for us," Violet answered matter-of-factly.

Rosalie leaned against the mantle again. "That won't last. We can't expect them to take care of us forever."

Violet's fists went to her hips. "I don't see why not. They want us here after all. It seems they're desperate for women, and I bet they'll be willing to pay."

This could quickly get out of hand. "While both of you have valid points, the sheriff did mention that the town was only willing to help us temporarily. Besides, we have a way of supporting ourselves. The mine. Ivan was able to get enough money from it to build this house. He was also able to send for each of us, and I don't know about all of you, but he was generous with his money in sending for me." The women all nodded. "It seems like we need to mine."

Willow held up her satin skirts. "You don't really expect us to do the labor, do you? I mean, I'm not afraid to work if it needs to happen, but there has to be another way."

"Why don't we hire someone?" Belle pipped in.

Juliette looked to Clara with calm, intelligent eyes. "She's right. This is a town full of miners, after all."

Aria shrugged as she lounged unladylike in her chair. "Makes sense to me. I don't know the first thing about mining."

"I don't think any of us do," Olivia added softly.

Rosalie paced the rug in front of the fire. "But how much would that cost us? We have no idea how long it would take for the mine to produce anything. I have a little of what Ivan gave to me, but not much. We wouldn't be able to pay someone… unless someone here has money they're not telling the rest of us about." She eyed Violet suspiciously.

Violet's lips twisted into a smile, but she remained silent.

Willow interrupted the silent battle. "We need help. It makes the most sense to hire someone from town who knows what they're doing. Perhaps we could offer them a percentage of what they find instead of paying a wage. It's riskier for them, but they'd be motivated to find gold."

Rosalie nodded at Willow. "I like that idea. It's the best option by far."

"Would anyone else like to offer a suggestion?" Clara asked.

The room was silent as a few shook their heads.

"All right then. I'll go to town tomorrow and find someone if there aren't any objections." When no one argued, she continued, "With that handled, we need to figure out sleeping arrangements. I was speaking with the sheriff and didn't get a look around. Does anyone know how many bedrooms there are?"

"Five," Sadie said. "But only eight beds."

Violet shook her head. "I will *not* sleep on the floor."

Willow sneered at the selfish statement. "Would it kill you to not be so self-centered for five minutes? No one said you had to. There's nine of us here. We can draw straws, and the person with the short straw has to sleep on the floor for the night. I'm sure we can arrange for a bed to be delivered tomorrow."

"That's fair," Aria agreed.

Belle shrugged. "One night won't kill us. The nights during our travels here couldn't have been any more comfortable than that."

Sadie quietly left the room and returned a moment later with straws from a broom she must have found during her tour of the house. She offered them to Clara. "Why don't you handle the drawing?"

Clara's hands closed over the prickly items. She was weary from traveling, but she had spent more nights on the floor than she could count. With eleven siblings, beds were a luxury. Besides, the final bed would be there tomorrow, and they'd all be comfortable then. From everyone's appearances, they were as weary as she, and several of them looked like they'd led very comfortable lives up until that moment.

She wasn't responsible for Ivan's deception, but she was here now, and she had promised to help the women get settled. She intended to help them all she could.

Clara placed the straws down on the seat beside her. "We don't need to draw. I'll take the floor tonight."

"That's not right," Sadie objected, and it was the first burst of light Clara had seen in the woman's eyes. "We should draw."

Violet's gazed cut the girl down. "If she's willing to sleep on the floor, let her."

Sadie's eyes immediately lowered, but she shook her head and looked up, glaring as if upset with both Violet and herself for cowering.

"Everyone stay calm." An ache formed behind Clara's eyes, and she wanted this all decided so she could rest. "I don't mind sleeping on the floor. To be honest, I've slept on the floor a good portion of my life, and doing it for one more night won't hurt me. As we've already stated, a bed can probably be delivered tomorrow. This really isn't a big deal."

Juliette's almost black eyes met hers. "If you're sure."

"I am." Clara sucked in a deep breath and looked at each of the women's faces. So different, each of them. It was as if Ivan wanted a variety of women to choose from. She frowned. He probably had. "So, we'll need to figure out a rotation for meal preparation—"

"Actually," Olivia interrupted, "there's a cook and a maid. Ivan paid them in advance for the month last week, and they're willing to continue on and earn the wages he gave them."

Clara's mouth fell open. A cook and maid? What on earth was she going to do all day? If they weren't cooking, cleaning, or mining—they'd be courting. Of course. "Well, all right then. If there isn't anything else pressing, I suggest we end the meeting and talk more again tomorrow after I've gone to town. Agreed?"

Most women nodded while others sounded their agreements vocally.

"Good. With any luck, the mine will produce a tidy sum for us, giving us plenty of time to choose husbands for ourselves."

"Here, here!"

The joyous calls warmed her heart. She was doing something good by helping these women. Ivan had deceived them all, but they could make the best of a bad situation.

They were housed, warm, and the future was open. The world looked bright, all right.

Chapter Five

Sawyer knew the minute he stepped out of his office at the jail the next morning, he was about to make a mistake, but that didn't deter him. If heading over to Ivan's place was a misstep, it was one he was determined to make.

It was his duty to check on the women, he assured himself. They were alone. New. Someone should look in on them. His decision to visit them had absolutely nothing to do with seeing Clara again.

Nothing.

He'd have to be dead not to be attracted to her, but he refused to do anything about it. Taking one of the brides for himself would cause a riot. He could just imagine hot-headed miners stabbing him with pick axes if they thought he'd swindled them out of a prize.

And Clara Stewart was definitely a prize.

The way her eyes had glowed with intelligence

and compassion yesterday, taking charge of the situation regardless of the distress she must have felt, lured him. The gumption she possessed was sexy as hell.

As he rode toward their property, his heart sped as quickly as Strike's pace beneath him. He shouldn't want to see her again, damn it. But he couldn't help it. She made him feel alive.

He dismounted at Ivan's house, whistling with the birds in the early morning light. Dew coated every surface, but the droplets only seemed to enhance the air's wildflower perfume instead of dampening it. He felt good. Life *was* good.

Swaggering up the stone steps, he knocked briskly at the door. Ivan's maid wasn't old, exactly, but when it took a moment for the door to open, he hadn't been surprised.

"Hello Sylvia, I'm here to see…" When a very scraggly Clara finished opening the door, her frown heavy enough to scare away the fiercest men in his jail, his jaw almost dropped. Her hair would make some lucky rat completely at home. "What happened? Are you all right?" Had something happened to her?

He stepped into the house, not bothering with etiquette. He scouted their surroundings until he was sure she was safe and then gripped her chin so he could get a good look at her. "Did something happen last night? Did someone bother you? You're not hurt are you?"

She swatted his hand. "I'm fine."

She stepped away from him, but her surly tone didn't mask the dark smudges under her eyes. "What happened?"

She scrubbed a hand over her face, summoning rosy splotches. "I guess I look worse than I thought." When he refused to take her bait, she sighed and lifted her hands. "Nine women. Eight beds."

His brows lowered. "And you slept where exactly?" he asked, but the answer was obvious.

"The settee. Although I would've been better off sleeping on the floor," she grumbled.

Why that answer infuriated him was beyond him. "Why didn't you send for a bed? I told you we'd get you anything you needed."

One of her hips popped out in a huff. "Because it was too late to send for one. Besides, it was just for a night. I was planning on coming into town later this morning to have one delivered."

"No need. I'll make sure one is sent over and save you a trip." He couldn't keep them in the house forever. He knew that, but having a few more days to get the town acclimated to the idea of nine marriageable women and the boundaries the men needed to obey would be helpful.

"Thank you. I have other business I need to see to in town, but having that off my list of things to do is helpful. I don't relish the idea of spending another night on *that*." She glared at the offending piece of furniture.

"What other things? I could take care of them for you. There's no need to rush to do anything. It's best if you take a few days to recover from your travels."

Her lips quirked. "I've never taken time to recover from much of anything. But in any case, this is something I need to do personally. The other women and I have decided to find someone to help with the mine. We're all extremely unqualified and would probably do more harm than good."

Shock warred with anger. "And how are you going to go about finding help?" Had she no idea how many men would kill to get their hands on Ivan's stake? Granted, it had never paid big and likely never would, but that wouldn't stop money-grabbing prospectors from ruthless tactics to get their hands on it. And they had plenty of those types in town. They'd devour her and swindle her out of the mine before she could blink.

"I figured I'd ask around. There has to be people interested in a job."

Sawyer closed his eyes and counted to ten before speaking. "And where exactly would you start asking around?"

"The mercantile? The barber shop? I don't know. Around. I figured I'd see what was in town and go from there." She frowned, finally giving him her full attention. "Why are you breathing like that? Is something wrong?"

Obviously deep breaths weren't helping. "Do you have any idea what type of men you'll find there? You'll be taken advantage of before you open your mouth."

Her back straightened. "I absolutely will not. I'm not a fool. I've dealt with men plenty of times in my life before, thank you."

She might have spoken with men from the east, but she'd never had to handle roughnecks from the west. "I can't allow you to do that. If you need help with the mine, I will help you find someone."

"No, thank you."

"No, thank you?" He gaped. Had she no sense of self-preservation at all? "That wasn't a request, Miss Stewart. I'm telling you flat out not to go into town and hire someone. No good will come of it."

Her eyes narrowed. "The last I checked, you were neither my father nor husband. You have no right to order me about. I'm capable of seeing to this task, and I intend to."

"That may be so," he ground out, more angered by the fact that she was right. He never would be her husband. He'd never have the right to protect her or see to her welfare. "But I'm the sheriff here, and I'm the law. You'd do best to remember that."

"Oh, I think it'll be impossible to forget." She yanked the door open. "Now, if you'll excuse me, I have some things to do."

Sawyer smashed his hat back on his head and headed out the door. "I'll be sure to have a bed sent over immediately. Let me know if there's anything else you need."

Her answer was the door closing behind him.

He cursed as he mounted Strike. What was wrong with him? He was a great sheriff because he was smooth in every situation. He used strength, sweet-talked when needed, and maneuvered others when necessary. But he'd never lost his temper, had never mishandled a situation.

But that's exactly what he'd done.

Clara Stewart deserved an apology. He had no right ordering her about, regardless of the dangers he saw. He might be the sheriff, but he had no rights over her as she'd said. The next time he saw her, he'd fix this.

He had to. He had a feeling the women would need his help even more than he first thought.

Heaven help him.

"ARE YOU SURE THIS IS the right way to go about it?" Belle stood with Clara in the middle of the road as they stared at the saloon's doors. The sun was starting to set, and while they had enough light to make it home, they shouldn't dawdle after their task was finished.

The town was small compared to the cities back east, but it was expanding and already boasted more buildings and business than other western communities she'd passed on her travels.

Clara squashed the flutter of unease in her belly. "I don't see a way around it. We need to find someone to work the mine. The sooner the better. There's a bunch of men in there." Never in her wildest dreams had she imagined barging into a saloon.

Belle bit her bottom lip. "Perhaps we should've listened to Sheriff Morrison. He knows the people in this town. Maybe we should ask him for his help in finding a miner."

The truth of Belle's words burned Clara's already raw pride. The fact that she even contemplated going into the saloon let her know just how far she'd gone. No respectable woman would set foot in there. "We can't wait for the sheriff to handle this.

We need money. The sooner we find someone to work the mine, the less pressure there will be on all of us to marry quickly. Everyone is counting on me. I said I would find someone, and I will."

Picking up her skirts, Clara steered clear of mud puddles in the road and stepped onto the boardwalk outside the saloon.

She gasped as the doors opened and a man flew out, landing just beside her.

"Sleep it off, Bob," the man who did the throwing said before going back inside without even glancing in her direction.

Bob groaned on the thick planks, but didn't move. A moment later, he snored.

Clara rolled her eyes heavenward. This was what it had come to. Her standing outside a place she shouldn't be with a drunk asleep at her feet.

She darted a glance at Belle who only gave her a concerned smile.

I hope I'm making the right choice. But even as she thought it, she knew she was. The others were depending on her. She couldn't let them down.

Steeling her resolve, she pushed open the saloon doors, but stopped dead in her tracks, unable to cross the threshold. Smoke curled in the air from the men's cigars at a corner table, their concentration focused on the card game in progress. Bawdy laughter abraded her ears and glasses clinked as men drank small shots of amber liquid.

"Um. Excuse me." Her voice was lost in the chaos. "Excuse me," she said a little louder, but no one paid her any attention.

She'd been nervous over this? She was certain

her presence would cause a commotion, but no one even cared. The sheriff had gotten upset over nothing.

While she felt more relaxed than before, she still couldn't bring herself to actually take a step into the establishment. Too many years of her mother's rules about proper etiquette for a young lady stopped her from going in.

A large man to her left laughed loudly and backed into her. "Get out of my way," he said before turning. He almost jumped out of his skin when he saw whom he'd bumped into.

"I beg your pardon." Clara's cheeks flushed with color at his scolding. She *was* blocking the door, after all.

He immediately ripped the hat off his head and held it to his chest. "No need. I didn't realize who was behind me."

Clara smiled at his attempt at manners. Perhaps not all the men here were as rough as she'd first thought. She was about to further converse with him when she realized the room had gone silent.

Slowly glancing around, she noticed everyone stared. At her.

Her cheeks grew hotter.

No one spoke. No one even moved. Heavens, this *had* been a mistake. But she still needed to hire someone, and she'd already made a spectacle of herself. She might as well follow through.

She cleared her throat. "I'm sorry to disturb you all." She ignored a guffaw from someone at the bar. "But I'm new in town and am looking to hire someone to work our mine."

A man jerked up from a chair, swaying with the sudden movement. "I'll do its," he slurred.

"No. I will," another man declared.

Clara glanced around frantically as more men agreed to work for her. "Thank you, but—"

A man who's smell would raise the dead gripped her arm and yanked her into the bowels of the saloon. "You'll want to hire me for the job. Let's go to a room to discuss this privately."

The stench that floated out from his mouth when he grinned with rotted teeth almost knocked her over. It was then she realized that it was one of the men from yesterday. The one that'd claimed her. Simon.

She tried to free her arm from his grasp. "No, I–"

"Let go of her." Another man jumped in to defend her, wrenching her arm as he grabbed the man holding her.

She cried out, her arm throbbing from being ripped from the man's grip and then grabbed by two more. "Stop! Let me go!" she screamed as the men used her as the rope in a game of tug-of-war.

A fight broke out in front of her. Wild punches flew inches from her face. Fear laced through her, thick and deadly. Entering the saloon doors had seemed so harmless, but now, she'd be lucky to make it out of the building without severe injury.

A gun shot rang through the air, and the room jerked to a stand still.

Footsteps sounded behind her through the saloon doors. "I think the lady already asked to be released."

Clara closed her eyes in relief.

Sawyer.

Regardless of what had happened that morning, she was relieved he was there.

Once meaty hands released her arms, she scurried in reverse until her back connected with Sawyer's chest.

"Are you all right?" he whispered in her ear.

She'd never been pressed up to a man before, but she couldn't even think about it. She was just grateful for his presence, for his protection. And with him there, behind her, she knew no one would hurt her. "I'm all right. You got here just in time."

She felt his slow nod, and she shivered. If he hadn't gotten there when he had…

One of the men finally snapped out of it and pushed his way forward. "Now see here. You've gots no right comin' in here and shootin' up the place. That woman is up for grabs." More men vocalized their agreement and began rustling again. "And I intend to have one. Move aside."

More cheers echoed through the group as they surged forward.

Sawyer gripped Clara's shoulder and maneuvered her behind him. "Take Belle and go back home."

She didn't argue.

"Be careful," she whispered and ran from the saloon, both worried and thankful Sawyer had been there.

As she and Belle raced back to the house, she wondered when she'd stopped thinking of him as the sheriff and just as Sawyer.

But even more, she wondered what thinking of

him as a man meant.

She was afraid to find out.

Chapter Six

When Belle had raced into his office and told him what was happening in the saloon, Sawyer felt his first real zing of panic. But none of that compared to the rage he felt when he'd walked through the door and witnessed two lowlifes ripping her apart.

Now, with her out of harms way, he stared down the volatile crowd. Insults were thrown at him as he blocked the door, giving the women more time to leave.

Red-hot fury slowly cooled to a numbness he welcomed. "I'm afraid there's been a misunderstanding here. The women are not up for grabs."

"Then why are they here? They're brides, aren't they?" The questions set off more rounds of rants and threats.

"If you would've come to the town meeting, you'd know. They came to marry Ivan. However, now that Ivan died, Mayor Bracken made them a deal that they would have Ivan's mine and house if all nine women agreed to stay and be courted. *Courted*," he said again, stressing the word. "Not manhandled, bullied, claimed, or anything else. The women are the one's with the choice in the matter. If any of you want to take one of them to wife, you'll have to get them the old-fashioned way. Woo them."

Simon sneered. "But how's that gonna work? There's more than nine men that want wives. I'm not willin' to take the chance I won't get one."

Sawyer's eyes narrowed as he rested a hand on his weapon, threatening the man for the second time in forty-eight hours. "And what exactly are you going to do?"

"Make one marry me."

"Listen to me." Sawyer looked around the room and made sure he had each and every man's attention. "If I hear of one of the women being mistreated as I witnessed in here today, or if any of them are threatened or pressured into marriage, there'll be hell to pay. The women were given my word that they'd be protected. So help me if you make me a liar."

"You can't stop us from marrying them," another called from the bar.

"I'm not trying to. All I'm doing is making sure they're won fairly and married to men of their choosing. If any of you are unwilling to take the time to court them, you're welcome to send off for a mail-order bride of your own as you've always been."

Grumbles sounded, and a few glares were tossed his way, but no one else argued. Not even Simon. That only made Sawyer more unsettled. It should've been harder to wrangle the men.

As he thought of what he'd witnessed when he'd first walked in, he backed out of the saloon before he did something really stupid. Like shooting them all.

Things were turning out worse than he'd imagined and additional safeguards would need to be put in place to ensure the women's safety. But what else could be done? They'd been removed from the town and put on another property.

They could post a guard outside the house, but who could he trust to handle such a task? Every single man in town was looking for a wife. Having the women completely at one man's disposal was dangerous, but it was also unfair. There'd be no end of complaints when someone got extra time to get to know the women.

Besides, who was capable enough? Certainly not any of the drunks back at the saloon. Whoever was put in charge of the women needed to be honest, respect the law, and have the means to defend them.

But as Sawyer mulled over the limited options in town, he slowly came to one glaring conclusion.

He was the only choice.

The men that had the means to protect them couldn't be trusted, and the ones he knew that respected the law, weren't skilled enough to ward off unwanted suitors.

Damn. It had to be him.

He rubbed the back of his neck as he strode to

the jail to pack his bags. Whether he wanted to or not, his job had gotten a lot more complicated.

He couldn't leave the women on their own. No matter how much he had to sacrifice, and torturing himself by constantly being by Clara's side without touching her was a sacrifice.

But he couldn't allow them to go unprotected.

He shoved clothes into a sack faster as an image of his mother came to mind. He hadn't been there the day she was attacked, but he replayed the scene over and over in his mind. Her, forced into an alley at gun point, and his father going in after her to save her.

He never saw the gun before her attacker shot him. The police found his mother's body next to his father's.

Sawyer's nostrils flared as he yanked the sack closed.

No one would ever suffer what his parents had as long as he lived.

❧

CLARA WASN'T ABOVE ADMITTING when she was wrong. And perhaps she'd been wrong about going into town yesterday. Sawyer *had* warned her that it wasn't a good idea.

Actually, he forbade it, her mind taunted, but Clara continued to make her new bed. What's done is done. She'd made a decision, it was the wrong one, and—and she'd almost gotten into serious trouble.

She sunk down on the patchwork quilt, tuning

out an argument between Violet and Willow in the next room. If Sawyer hadn't come when he had—she shivered—God only knew what would've happened to her.

Her arms ached where she'd been stretched and pulled like taffy.

She should've been safe surrounded by all those people. But she wasn't.

What was she going to do? They couldn't stay locked up in the house forever.

She'd have to be much more careful next time. Not take any chances.

New policies would have to be created to keep them all safe.

She sighed, guessing some of the women would love the restrictions as much as a hearty dose of Castor oil. That was exactly how Clara felt about such limitations.

A knock sounded at the door. "Clara?"

"Yes? Come in."

Olivia opened the door, lingering in the frame instead of entering. The reserved, delicate woman watched her with kind, indigo eyes.

"Sounds like we're about to have another civil war out there," Clara said, trying to lighten the mood. Olivia was one of the quieter women, but she saw more. Felt more. Some people were just blessed with that ability.

Olivia chuckled. "Those two seem to have gotten off on the wrong foot."

"Tell me about it." Clara rolled her eyes. "If we all manage to stay alive until they're married, it'll be a miracle.

"If they get married."

Olivia's words set off alarm bells. "Of course they'll get married. That's what we've come here to do, isn't it?"

"A few of the women have mentioned that there wasn't a need to marry now that we have a way to support ourselves with the mine. We aren't as desperate as we were before."

Clara slowly leaned forward. "That's true. But we did give our word that we would allow men to court us."

"Yes. But courting and marrying are two different things.'"

Olivia had a point. If the mine was profitable, there was no rush to the alter.

A shriek echoed down the hall. "Oh, Lord, save us." Clara breathed deeply. "Was there something you needed?"

The woman's lithe back straightened. "I forgot. Sheriff Morrison is here to see you."

Clara's shoulders slumped. "Of course he is," she mumbled.

"What was that?"

"Nothing."

Olivia arched a brow.

"All right, fine. I might have made a mistake yesterday, and I'm sure he's here to rub my nose in it."

"I don't know him well, but I don't think he's the type of man to do that."

Clara would have said the same thing if she'd been an only child, but she had brothers aplenty. They never failed to rub any of their sisters' mistakes in their faces. "I guess we'll see."

Olivia discreetly left, allowing Clara a moment to freshen up before descending to the parlor. With each step she took, the nerves in her belly churned so by the time she walked into the room, she couldn't hold back her apology. "I'm so sorry I didn't listen to you. You were right that I shouldn't go into town alone. It was stupid and irresponsible, and I'm sorry," she rushed out and closed her eyes in relief. He could rub it in her face if he wanted to, but her conscious was clear.

When her eyes fluttered opened, he rocked back on his heels. "Feel better?"

A smile twitched at her lips before she grinned. "Much. I hate being wrong, but when I am, I like to get the apology out of the way fast."

He nodded once. "I wanted to talk to you about a guard for the house."

Her eyebrows shot up. "Really? You aren't going to say I told you so? Taunt me even a little?"

"When you just apologized so nicely?"

"You aren't that kind, are you? My brothers would've tormented me for days."

He muffled a laugh. "Brothers tend to do that."

"Do you have any? Brothers," she clarified. Suddenly needing to know more about him.

He nodded. "One. He doesn't live far from here, in fact. No more than five miles."

She swallowed hard. "It must be nice to have family close by. I miss mine."

"How many siblings do you have?"

"Eleven." His reaction brought a slow smile to her face. "Yes. A big family. I'm the oldest, and it was hard to leave."

"Why did you?"

She shrugged, trying to hide how much it still hurt. "I had to. Not enough food to go around."

He nodded grimly. "I understand. Clara, about yesterday—"

"I know it was foolish," she rushed out to say. "I see that."

"Why did you do it? I warned you it was dangerous."

She shuffled her feet before answering. "It's my responsibility."

"To do what?" His brows wrinkled in confusion, and Clara couldn't blame him. It was difficult for her to explain.

"I told the women that I'd help them, that I would do everything in my power to get them through this. If I have to sleep on the floor or take a risk by going into town, then so be it."

Frustration tinged her cheeks. She knew it sounded ridiculous, but he didn't have to look at her like she'd lost her mind.

She glared at him. "I don't expect you to understand."

He whistled. "I don't. I see that you want to protect them. I can see it's your nature, and after taking care of eleven siblings, even understandable. But you have to see that endangering your life isn't the right way to go about it."

She crossed her arms. "And I think it's none of your concern what I choose to do or why I choose to do it. I appreciate your assistance in the saloon earlier, and I can promise to try and be more careful in the future, but I will always do what I think is right."

"Even if it puts yourself at risk?"

"Even then."

He silently stared her down, but she wouldn't cower. He might as well learn that now. Once Clara decided something, she did it. And right now, she was determined to help those women. "Was there anything else you wanted to discuss, Sheriff Morrison?"

He turned his head and mumbled something she knew wasn't complimentary, but refused to ask him to repeat his answer.

"Yes," he finally said. "I wanted to come by after what happened and talk to you about extra precautions."

"I told you—"

"Not just for yourself, but for all the women. I originally thought you'd be safe out here alone, but after what happened, I'm not so confident anymore."

Her belly fluttered. She couldn't argue with him. "What do you suggest?"

"I think you should have a guard posted here at the house. Someone that could watch out for you and keep away amorous suitors unless specifically invited. They'd sleep in the barn or somewhere else where you'd hardly notice them."

It made sense. She would feel a lot more secure if there were someone looking out for them, but how could they trust someone they didn't know. "How would we pay this person? Surely they wouldn't do it for free."

His chin notched up. "I intend on doing it

myself, and I consider it part of my job. In fact, I slept in the yard last night just to make sure you all stayed safe. My salary is payment enough."

Shock laced through her. He'd slept in the yard all night? She didn't want to even contemplate why that made her heart race. "Why would you do that? Don't you have other things to do?" Her stomach fluttered again, but it wasn't from fear. She was afraid it was excitement.

What kind of person would she be if she let her infatuation for the sheriff, an exceptional, marriageable man, keep her from doing all that she could for the other women? A relationship with him would distract her.

He chuckled, his whole body loosening with the movement. "I have a feeling most of the men in town will only get into trouble over the women here. At least in the mean time. Mining, gambling, and drinking, let alone street fighting, have become old to them. You women are what's new and exciting."

As his gaze traveled over her, heat sprung to her cheeks. It was as if he was saying he found her exciting. But he couldn't possibly after what had happened in town, could he?

But for the moment, she relished the thought. What would it be like to have a man like him looking out for her? Wanting her? Needing her?

She shivered. The pleasure she derived from such thoughts overwhelmed her.

She knew that being wanted by Sawyer Morrison would be an experience unlike any other.

Chapter Seven

"Remember, the men are here by our invitation," Clara said, gazing at the group of women she slowly was getting to know. Aria, Willow, Rosalie, and Olivia seemed excited about the prospect of entertaining a large group of men, while Juliette and Sadie seemed concerned, maybe even a little overwhelmed. Violet was, well, Violet. "If anyone gets out of hand, let me know, and we'll have them escorted out."

When no one had any other questions, she nodded once. "Well, then, let's not keep our guests waiting. Do you all have your baskets?"

The picnic auction was a brilliant fundraising idea. Since they'd been unable to secure a worker for the mine, they were in need of cash. And what better way to raise money than to do it while fulfilling their end of the bargain?

"Shouldn't we wait for the sheriff?" Sadie asked.

Clara glanced out the window at the bustling

crowd. "I don't think we can. If we wait any longer, the men might decide to take matters into their own hands and break down the door."

Sadie's eyes rounded. "You don't think they will, do you?"

"No." Clara scolded herself once she saw Sadie's unease. "They wouldn't do that. They're here to win us over. They have to know it would never work. Besides, the sheriff is looking out for us. The men know that if they did anything untoward, he would make them pay. Regardless of whether he's here or not."

Her words appeased Sadie.

As the women exited the house through the back door, applause and excited whistles filled the air. Isabelle and Aria chuckled at the unrefined display while Violet's lip curled.

Heavens. If they made it through the picnic auction without Violet offending anyone, she'd call it a success.

In an array of different colored gowns, they lined up on the grass in front of the back porch. Thanks to Ivan, he'd provided enough money so that all of the women had new dresses for the wedding. And while they wouldn't be marrying Ivan in them, they were possibly meeting their future husbands in the fancy clothing he'd provided.

Clara stepped forward. "Thank you all for coming today." Another round of boisterous hollers rang her ears. She had to wait a full minute for the noise to die down. The crowd was even larger than she'd anticipated. "As you know, we came here to marry Ivan, but with his passing, we've been left in a rather difficult position. Without a means of fully supporting ourselves, we came up with this idea to not only raise funds, but to start the courting process as fairly as possible. Each woman, including myself, have a picnic basket that we packed to share with one companion."

A large man with a freshly shaved jaw and kind smile stepped forward. "How will the companions be decided?"

Clara was just about to explain that before the man's interruption, but she wouldn't scold him. He looked too nice for her to do such a thing. "Thank you for asking. Each basket will be auctioned off, and whoever purchases the basket will also win the company of the woman it belongs to. The winners will have exclusive time to get to know the women without interruption. Any questions?"

"Yes, ma'am." A man stepped forward, his manners and appearance like that of a gentleman back east. "How long will the exclusive time last?"

"Thirty minutes at least. Unless the man behaves improperly. The time will immediately be cut off then."

The crowd went quiet as they absorbed that heavy bit of information. She was suddenly grateful to the man for asking. "Any other questions?" She glanced around, but no one spoke. "Excellent. Then we'll start with the first basket." She looked toward the women, noting nerves, and decided to have Aria go first as she looked the most at ease. "Aria, please step forward."

Dimples winked in Aria's cheeks as she grinned at the crowd. "I think you'll like what I packed," she said with a wink.

Chuckles floated in the air.

Clara couldn't have been more pleased with the interest in the men's eyes. While there was strong prejudice against the Irish, she was happy that the men here didn't seem to mind Aria's heritage. "Let's start the bidding at a dime. Do I have a dime?"

A man quickly raised his hand.

"How about a quarter?" she asked, nodding at another man after he bid. "Fifty cents?"

"A dollar!" one of the men yelled, drowning her out.

"Dollar fifty," another called.

"Two dollars."

"Four!"

Clara reeled as the numbers climbed higher without her assistance. These men were even more aggressive—and rich—than she'd first realized. Wondering how Aria was taking it, she glanced over at her. Her mouth hung open, astounded by the interest in her.

To go from zero interest from men back home to this must be a shock.

As the bidding died down, Clara gathered her wits. "The bidding is at ten dollars. Do I hear ten-fifty? No? Ten dollars going once. Ten dollars going twice. Sold to the man in the black hat."

Men pounded the winner on the back in congratulations. The joviality was high since there were so many more baskets left, but Clara wondered if the friendliness would continue as the number of women dwindled. There had to be at least thirty men.

"Next up is Olivia." The blonde smiled shyly at the crowd. "Let's start the bidding at one dollar this time."

Each and every basket was auctioned off at well over what any of them had hoped for. And Clara was also relieved to note that each of the winners looked like gentlemen. At the high prices the baskets were going for, it was no wonder that the unkempt, rougher men couldn't afford one.

"And finally, we're left with my basket."

"The basket we've all been waiting for," the kind man in front said with a wink. The rest of the men called out encouragements.

Clara's cheeks pinked to the exact shade of her gown. She'd had her fair share of suitors, but none had seemed as serious in their pursuits as the men here today. "Why don't we start it off at the same amount as the others? Who'll bid one dollar?"

When the bidding rose to obscene amounts, finally ending at thirty-two dollars and fifty cents, she smiled at the disappointed crowd. "There's no need to be upset, gentlemen. Please stay and help yourselves to the refreshments laid out on the table over there. Once each couple has finished their lunches, there'll be plenty of time to mingle with all of the ladies.

The nice man up front who'd complimented her was the highest bidder, and Clara was pleased with how it all had turned out. "Your name, sir?"

He took off his hat and introduced himself. "Teddy Wallace, ma'am."

"Congratulations, Teddy." She smiled. "If you'll follow me to—"

"What the hell is going on here?"

Clara spun to find an angry Sawyer glaring at her. "Sawy—I mean sheriff, is there something I can do for you?"

As he stalked closer, his glare at Teddy forced the man a step away from her.

The nerve! Sawyer had no right to interfere here.

"You can start by telling me what on earth is going on. Why are all these men here, and what could possibly be going through that thick skull of yours to allow this to happen? Especially when I'm not here?"

Clara's smile tightened on her face. "Will you excuse us for a moment, Teddy?"

The man glanced between the sheriff and her. "No problem. I'll be waiting by that tree over there." He nodded off to his right, but she didn't look.

Sawyer gripped her arm and steered her away from the crowd. When they were around the side of the house and away from prying eyes, she ripped her arm out of his hold. "Don't you dare ever pull me aside again like some recalcitrant child, Sawyer. Next time, I won't be so accommodating."

His mouth fell open before snapping it closed. "You're upset with me? Woman, have you no sense at all? Do you not remember what happened in the saloon?"

"Of course I do! And this is nothing like that situation. In fact, I'm forced to do this because I was *unable* to find someone to work in the mine."

His jaw clenched, and she was happy her words hit their mark.

"I'll assume since you didn't inform me of this

gathering that you knew I wouldn't approve." He saw her guilty flush. "And you were absolutely right. I don't. There are far too many men here with only me for protection. I'm breaking this up immediately."

She gasped, reaching out to grip his arm. "I did tell you. I told you we were having a picnic today."

"You purposefully left out the part where men were invited."

"You can't send them home."

He took a step forward. "Yes. I can."

She shook her head wildly. Why was he behaving this way? There might be a lot of men here, but Clara was pretty sure if one behaved inappropriately, the others would bring the offender back in line. "We've already taken their money. How do you expect us to provide for ourselves if you won't allow us to do what we need to?"

He glanced at the couples picnicking around the perimeter of the group before locking eyes with her. "Once the couples have finished lunch, this is done. I want all of the women back in the house, secured while I make sure everything is safe. There are too many men here. Men I don't trust. I can't keep you safe in a crowd this large.

It almost killed Clara not to argue. She smiled tightly, hoping it would be enough to stop her from causing a scene. He might be in charge, but if Clara had learned anything from her family growing up, it was that there were other ways to get what she wanted.

Sawyer had no idea who he was dealing with.

SAWYER WATCHED CLARA AS SHE chatted prettily with Teddy under a willow tree, and fought the urge to go over and toss the man aside.

What on earth had gotten into him? How he'd behaved with Clara—again—was inexcusable. His only blessing was that his brother was purchasing new heads of cattle in Texas and wasn't there to mock him for his loss of control.

He glanced heavenward. Where was his easy-going nature now?

While he'd been a brute about it, he'd set out rules so Clara would be safe.

The women, he corrected. He'd done it so the *women* would be safe.

Not just Clara.

But he hadn't given a second glance to the other couples picnicking. In fact, it didn't bother him that they were sprinkled about, laughing and getting to know one another on this warm, spring day.

Was he… jealous?

Had he overreacted about the picnic because he couldn't stand the thought of Clara being with anyone but him? He gulped, accepting the truth. He thought he could stay away from her. That he could be objective. He obviously couldn't.

Teddy wasn't a bad man. In fact, he was a good match for any of the women. He was gentle, kind. And wealthy.

While he looked like any other man in a suit, Teddy had a profitable mine that had paid big throughout the years. His homestead was large, and his house massive.

And this was his opportunity.

Each and every man here wanted a woman. A wife. And they'd all fight to have one.

Sawyer might have a reprieve once the picnic was done, but he'd have to figure out some way to handle his emotions. Clara would marry. And he could never be her groom.

Not if he wanted to continue being sheriff in this town. If the men thought he'd stolen one of the women out from under them when he was supposed to be protecting them, the town would riot.

His body jerked when Teddy stood and helped Clara to her feet. Her smile was like a thousand candles in a dark room. Her warmth filled places in his soul that had long since gone dark.

Once again, the crowd gathered around her when she moved toward the house. "Thank you all for your patience. I think this activity has gone very well."

Whistles sounded the men's agreement.

She held up her hands. "Now, there's been a slight change of plans."

The group went silent, a few men glanced uneasily at Sawyer as he hovered to the side. It wouldn't have escaped their notice that he hadn't been there earlier. They had to wonder what changes he'd made.

Clara glanced to him. "Sheriff Morrison has been kind enough to point out some safety issues from this activity. Because of that, we've decided to finish the outside portion of today's events and—" she had to talk louder over their disappointments

"—and move the rest of the activity indoors. We'll be cramped, but we should all be able to manage to mingle throughout the first floor." She smiled ruefully. "Even if some of us end up in the kitchen."

She glanced over at Sawyer and it took all of his will power not to laugh.

The minx. She might be following his orders to get the women in the house, but she knew this was not what he'd meant.

He had to give it to her. She'd definitely won this round. And while it might be easier if she followed his orders, he was pleased that she had enough spirit to get what she wanted. She fascinated him. She was selfless and giving, but also strong. She didn't let others walk over her, and she found ways to get what she wanted.

That attitude would serve her well in the west.

It would also please her husband very much.

His hand clenched. The thought of anyone else enjoying her spirit did not sit well.

He followed closely behind her as she let the group into the house. She spoke briefly to the servants, no doubt telling them to bring the refreshments inside.

"Sylvia," he said, gaining the older woman's attention. "Will you do me a favor, and keep an eye on the ladies for a few moments?"

"Of course," she said, bustling off to handle both his and Clara's requests.

Clara's eyes widened as she quickly made her way to the kitchen. He followed her like a wolf hunting his prey, and she picked up her speed.

She twirled to face him once they were alone in

the kitchen as if she decided to fight rather than flee. "I did exactly as you said. You can't be upset about this, Sawyer." Color fled her cheeks. "I mean Sheriff Morrison."

Hearing his name on her lips did wicked things within him. His jealousy of the other men, and his amusement from her antics heated into something hot and achy. "I like it when you use my name."

She glanced to the doorway. "I'm not sure it's the best idea. It would be unseemly to become too familiar when I'm looking for a husband."

He took a step closer to her. She stepped back.

A grin quirked his lips. "Where are you going?"

"Away from you," she said, shivering as if she could already feel his touch.

"Are you afraid?"

"Of course not. You'd never hurt me."

It pleased him to hear her say so. "No. I would never hurt you nor any woman. But since we're on the subject, I want you to realize that there are other men out there that would."

"I know."

He paused the cat and mouse game. "If you do, then why did you invite them inside instead of asking them to leave? I know you understood what I meant earlier. This large of a crowd isn't safe with only me as protection."

She searched his eyes. "You'll keep us safe."

A surge of protectiveness rose through him. "I would certainly try. But what if someone cornered you?"

She shrugged as if that wasn't a problem. "That would never happen since I plan to never be alone with anyone."

"You could get caught unawares."

"I'm always careful."

He pounced on her, caging her against the kitchen table.

Her chest heaved against her corset. "What are you doing?" she whispered.

"Making a point." But even as he said it, he knew it was just an excuse to get closer to her. His hand rose up, and he stroked her cheek with an index finger.

Her lids closed heavily at his touch, and the small show of pleasurable acceptance made him crave more. "You weren't prepared for this."

Her eyes opened, unfocused and glazed. "No. No I wasn't."

"This could happen anywhere, at any time. You may think you're safe with these men, but you're not." He cradled her chin, searching her eyes for a sign that she didn't want his touch. "Tell me to stop. Tell me to move away."

Her mouth opened and closed. "I… I can't."

"You want this."

She bit her lip, nodding.

It was all he needed. Wrapping his free arm around her waist, he pulled her flush against him, relishing the visceral sensation of her body before he claimed her lips.

There wasn't a need to devour her, and he certainly didn't want to overwhelm her.

He sampled her slowly. A brush across her cheek, a fleeting caress on her jaw. He didn't leave a part of her exposed skin unclaimed.

He nuzzled her lips, rejoicing in her sigh of pleasure before he sampled her deeper. When she opened for him, his control almost snapped.

He kissed her harder, longer. Pulling out emotions, feelings, anything he could take from her. He needed this from her. Needed this connection. This sense of belonging.

In this moment, it didn't matter who was outside that door, who she'd speak to, or where she went. Because right now she was his. She belonged to him just as much as he did to her.

Their breath mingled as her hands trailed up his shirt, gripping his shoulders before winding around his neck. She held him tight as if she would never let go, and he felt the answering call within himself.

He pulled her tighter, trying to fuse their bodies as he kissed her with raw emotion. Never had anything felt so right. Never had he wanted another with such blazing intensity—

A cough sounded near the doorway.

They jerked apart, and he had a hard time clearing his head as he watched her touch her bruised lips.

He turned to the intruder and felt zero guilt at having kissed Clara.

"Should I come back in a few minutes?" Belle asked, trying not to smile.

He could just imagine what she was thinking. "No. I think Clara and I have said everything that needs saying."

Belle laughed then. From the looks of things, he and Clara had verbally discussed very little. Instead, they'd allowed their bodies to do most of the talking. "I'll be in the parlor watching over the group. Let me know if there's anything either of you need."

"We will," Clara finally said, nodding with an uncertain smile.

As he walked out of the room, he grinned. While nothing had changed, the group of men didn't seem to bother him as much.

Nope. Life sure looked great right now.

Chapter Eight

While the picnic was a success, two days later, Clara knew the money would only last so long with nine women in the house.

"Sawyer, may I have a moment of your time?" she asked, hovering in the kitchen doorway.

He wiped sweat off his brow and put down the ax he'd been using to chop firewood. While others could take over the task, she was grateful for his help.

And the sight of him, stripped down to a thin cotton shirt, his bared tanned skin slick with perspiration made her stomach flip in the most pleasant way. If she wasn't already familiar with feelings of attraction, she might've worried she was coming down with a stomach bug.

In the two days since the picnic, she'd become more and more obsessed with watching him. She couldn't help herself. Who could? She certainly caught a few of the other women glancing his way when he performed some physical task.

He was a handsome man.

But when their gazes lingered a little too long, that was when it became a problem for her. She'd already established that she couldn't marry him. At least not until all the others were married, and that didn't seem like it would happen anytime soon.

Clara led him into the parlor, lecturing herself, and offered him a cold glass of water and a sandwich. He accepted with a grateful nod before digging in. Her mother had taught her from a young age that it was best to ask a man for something after his stomach was full.

"What can I do for you?" he asked between bites.

You could kiss me again for starters. She coughed. "I um… was hoping to talk to you about our mine." When his chewing slowed, she held up her hands. "Now, before you end the discussion, I'd like you to hear me out."

"All right."

"Thank you." When he finished the sandwich, she offered him the plate. He was steadily working on the second when she continued. "I recognize I made a mistake the day I went into town looking for help. It was naive to think I would be able to find a gentleman and convince him to work for us. It was foolish, and I want you to know that I learned my lesson."

Her words put him at ease. "I'm glad to hear that. I'm sorry if I was rough with you that day. Something snapped when I saw the way you were being treated."

It must've taken a lot for him to admit such a

thing. In her experience, men didn't vocalize such emotions unless they were forced, and the fact that he did, softened her even more toward him. "I understand. And while I won't put myself in harms way again," she refused to point out the lesson he'd given her in the kitchen during the picnic, "we're still in need of someone to either work in the mine or teach us how so we can support ourselves."

"I could look around for a good fit. It might take me some time."

She placed her hand on a side table. "You see, I think I might've found someone already."

He put the sandwich down and leaned forward. "Who?"

"Well… you."

"Me? You want me to help you work your mine?"

"Or you could teach us how," she rushed to say. "I know you and your brother had a claim."

He shook his head and laughed. "I beg your pardon, Miss Stewart, but I'm not sure all of the ladies are up to such a task."

"Clara," she said quietly, watching through her lashes for his reaction.

He stilled. "What?"

"Clara. It's my Christian name. I'd like you to use it."

"Why?"

She swept her fingers over the table as if hunting dust. "Because. I call you Sawyer now. I feel like we've developed some type of friendship. It feels odd to have you address me as Miss Stewart."

Silence lingered in the air. "I thought it was

unseemly."

She shrugged, refusing to give away her feelings.
"What do you want from me?"

"I told you. To help us learn to mine," she said, but knew that wasn't what he meant. The truth was, she didn't know what she wanted from him. Part of her longed for him to take her into his arms, but that wasn't possible.

He nodded slowly as he stood from his seat. "All right."

She perked up. "You will?"

"Until I can find someone to work the mine, someone who can be trusted, I'll teach you. It's not work I enjoy, but I'll show you how to do it."

Breath whooshed from her chest. Her shoulders sagged. Finally, she'd secured something to help their future. This was a huge first step toward making them self-sufficient. If they could make the mine profitable, she and all the other women would have plenty of time to marry.

Excitement bubbled within her. She'd helped the women just as she'd said. She'd made that happen.

And Sawyer fulfilled that.

She jumped from her chair and launched herself into his arms. "Thank you!"

He chuckled, then wrapped his arms around her, squeezing. "You're welcome."

His breath fanned hotly against her neck, and she shivered. She didn't move, couldn't bring herself too. Being held in his arms felt so right. So good. She wasn't alone. He was with her, sharing her burden of helping the women. She'd always had her family to rely on, but they weren't here now.

His hands rubbed up and down her back slowly as if he was learning the feel of her, and she arched unconsciously into the touch.

"You're so beautiful, Clara."

His words ripped her from the sultry haze of his caresses.

She leaned away, but he held her firm.

She didn't try to move again as he searched her eyes. What was he looking for?

He must understand that there could be nothing between them right now. She enjoyed spending time with him, but he was also a distraction. "I… Thank you for helping in the mine."

He nodded once. "It's no problem. Mining is hard work though. I'm not sure you'll be thanking me after we're done."

"I'm not as weak as all that."

He slid an arm from around her waist up to her bicep and squeezed. "No. You're quite the prizefighter aren't you?"

A reluctant smile crossed her lips. "I might not be at a prizefighter's level, but I'm sure with hard work, I'll gain the muscle necessary."

"That's true." He frowned. "And while I'm willing to show you and the women how to find gold, there's some things that I won't allow you to do."

Her frown was back. "Why not?"

"It's too dangerous."

"Let me guess. Too dangerous for women?" she asked distastefully. Why did everyone think women weren't capable of things men were?

He shook his head. "Some things are dangerous

for everyone. Both men and women."

His words appeased her feminine outrage. At least he recognized that men had limits as well. "If we aren't able to do it all, how will we get by?"

"I'll find someone for you. Hopefully to do it all, but if not, I know I'll be able to get someone for the dangerous aspects. If anything," he said with a grin, "men would be willing if it meant being in your good graces."

"Is that all it takes to be in our good graces?"

"It'd be worth a try."

He released her, and she suddenly wished she was still held in his arms, regardless of the impossibility of it all.

He walked to the door, and her eyes trailed him.

"Talk to the others, and let them know the change in plans. Once they've agreed to my help, we can get started."

"Thank you."

His gaze caressed her face. "Don't thank me yet. You're sure to regret your choice to mine."

Her chin notched up. "I doubt that."

He chuckled as he walked out.

It couldn't be as bad as all that.

<hr />

"WHAT DO YOU MEAN WE have to work the mine ourselves?" Violet's lips pressed together.

Clara held up her hands to calm the group. "Please, everyone calm down. Lower your voices."

How was she in this same position, refereeing the group? Each of them couldn't seem to keep their temper in check each and every time they met together to make decisions. In truth, she was starting to dread these meetings.

Their personalities were too different. Out of the nine women, no two were alike. While variety was all well and good, it made tough living arrangements.

"Sheriff Morrison was kind enough to agree to show us how to work the mine."

Rosalie paced the rug as if moving fueled her thoughts. "What happened to hiring someone?"

Clara sighed. It really would've been so much easier if she'd been able to find someone. "The sheriff has pointed out that we can't blindly hand things over to a stranger. There are many people that would take advantage and try to steal the mine from us." That bit of news sobered the group. "He told me that while he is looking for someone to help us, he'd show us how to work it ourselves so we can start earning money immediately."

Willow lounged in a delicate silk gown. "Then why not wait until someone can be found? Why jump into mining ourselves when it will only last a short while? This is a mining town after all. Seems like a waste of time to me."

Several of the women nodded in agreement.

Did they not understand the situation they were in? But as Clara looked around at each of them, she concluded that most of them probably didn't. By their dress and what she'd heard of their backgrounds, several of them were from well-to-do families. They probably never had to work a day in their lives. But as she met the eyes of Aria, Belle, and Sadie, she saw that there were at least a few of them who knew what needed to be done.

"It may take some time to find someone. While this is a mining town, most of the men have moved on to other businesses after their mines paid out, and the ones that are left are working their own mines, trying to strike it rich. There aren't a lot of floating miners out of work here. To get someone to help us, we're going to have to make it worth their while."

Violet shook her head. "I'm not handing over a piece of the mine to someone else. I already have to split it with eight others."

Annoyed looks were tossed at the sharped-tongued woman. They all had to share the mine with each other.

"Listen," Clara's shoulders drooped, exhausted from the continual fight, "the sheriff won't allow us to do anything dangerous. We may get a little dirty and break a nail or two, but isn't it worth it so we can be independent? The town could get sick of supporting us at any moment. I for one, would hate to go without the cook and maid. Let alone go hungry because we can't afford to buy food."

Violet huffed. "They would never let that happen to us."

"Are you willing to bet on that? I'm not." She looked at the rest of the women. "I know this isn't ideal. I know that you all want to focus on courting and getting married, but this is a necessity. If it would make you all feel better, I'm happy to have Sheriff Morrison teach me how, and I'll evaluate to see if it's feasible for us to do so."

A few girls voiced their agreement.

Willow stood from the couch and nodded. "I guess we're mining." She fingered her satin skirts. "If this works out, we'll need to find appropriate garments. It wouldn't due to waste our own clothes on the endeavor."

Olivia smiled shyly. "If this goes well, we'll be able to afford as many gowns as we want."

Belle chuckled and laughter quickly flowed out of Aria's lips until the whole group was laughing.

Clara glanced around at the group of women who should've never even known each other, but were slowly becoming friends.

They were going to be all right.

Chapter Nine

Clara glanced skeptically at the river before turning back to Sawyer. "I thought you were going to teach me how to mine."

"Baby steps. Before we teach you to run, let's teach you to crawl." He grinned devilishly. "You'll want to tie up your skirts."

"You're kidding." She eyed the muddy riverbank. Not that she was afraid to get a little dirty, but tying up her skirts was not appropriate in mixed company. Oh, who was she kidding? It was never appropriate.

He loosely folded his arms. "You'll have to unless you want your dress ruined. You're going to need to bend over the river to rinse the soil. You can't pan for gold without water."

Clara chewed her lip. Panning was a legitimate way of finding gold. She could even find some her first time around. But tying up her skirts?

She glanced at Sawyer and the merriment

crinkling his eyes. The scoundrel! He knew she was struggling with her modesty.

Well—her chin notched up—if he was enjoying her discomfort, it was high time she made him uncomfortable too. Attraction had been simmering between them for far too long, and honestly, it was making her edgy. Perhaps torturing him would give her a little relief.

Holding up her skirts, she pushed them between her legs, dividing the fabric before crossing the yards of material back in front of her and tying the two sections into a solid knot. Something worthwhile *had* come out of climbing trees with her siblings. The shock on Sawyer's face as he stared at her stocking-clad legs made enduring all of her mother's lectures about the inappropriateness of climbing trees worth it.

She arched a brow at him. "Something the matter?"

He cleared his throat and brought his eyes up to hers. She grinned at the difficulty he seemed to have masking his emotions.

"No." He shook his head before grabbing a pan. "You just surprised me."

"Oh?"

"I wouldn't have expected a lady like you from the east to be able to manage that as quickly as you did."

"I'm not a lady." And that was the sorry truth. She wasn't refined, delicate. She'd worked her whole life, had scrimped and saved and went hungry to help her family. She would be working her fingers raw in a factory now if it wasn't for

Ivan's advertisement. Her shoulders slumped, and she looked at the clear, flowing water at her feet.

"You are to me."

He hadn't moved before saying those words. He hadn't reach out his hand. But even though he wasn't physically touching her, those small little words felt like a caress. "Dressed like this?" No lady would be caught dead with her skirts up.

Her eyes met his as he nodded. "It doesn't matter what you're wearing, Clara. You're a lady. You're gentle, kind. You look out for others, and you try to do the right thing. That makes you a lady in my book more than wearing a fancy get up and lifting your nose while quoting French poetry."

She could see it in his eye. He meant it. Every word.

Her heart beat a little faster. Her breath shallowed. He valued her. Thought she was more than a poor girl one step from starving, more than a pathetic woman duped into traveling hundreds of miles from her home, and more than the partially educated woman she believed herself to be.

Why did she continue to push this man away?

She thought she had to remain separate for the sake of the group. That somehow, if she got involved romantically, she wouldn't be able to help the other women. But that couldn't be farther from the truth. She saw that now.

Sawyer was already there. He was helping the women just as much as she was. Being with him wouldn't change that. There'd be some things they'd need to work out, but none of it was insurmountable.

Why shouldn't she have the opportunity to love and be loved? She'd come here to get married just like any of the other eight women. If she was the first to find it, so what?

As she looked at Sawyer, really looked at him, her gaze lingering on the golden highlights the sun teased from his grown out hair, the way his linen shirt clung to harden muscles as he bent over the river, the way his pants showcased a rather attractive backside, she'd admitted that she'd never seen a more attractive man.

She blushed.

She shouldn't be noticing his backside. But she did. Right now, as the wind whistled softly in the trees and the stream bubbled lazily down the rocky bed, she took in everything about him.

She wanted him. Really wanted him. But did he want her?

Running a wet hand through his hair, making the tawny strands darker, he turned toward her with a smile. "You ready to start?"

Oh, was she ever. He had no idea she was about to make a play for his heart.

BREATH CAUGHT IN HIS THROAT as he turned toward Clara after testing the water temperature. There was something different in her eyes, something smoldering. And she was looking at him.

She walked toward him, her hips swiveling as she got closer to the water's edge. "What do I do first?" Her voice was breathy as if winded from exertion, and a shiver raced down his spine.

It was how she sounded after a kiss. His kiss.

"You'll need a pan. Grab the extra one out of the sack." He gestured to the brown bag on the ground, hoping she didn't hear the edge in his voice.

"This one?" She held up a dingy pan he'd used for years.

"Yep." She moved next to him, and her shoulder brushed against his arm. He cleared his throat. "So, ah, there's not much to panning for gold if you know what you're doing and what to look for. Gold was plentiful here, so it's possible that you could find some in any spot on the river, but the best places to look are where the gold could get caught over time."

"Caught?" Her brows wrinkled so adorably, he wanted to kiss the puckered skin.

He stopped himself before moving in. Barely. "Gold is heavier than rocks and silt. So if you can find places where stuff get's caught in cracks or dips, you're likely to find better deposits. But for the sake of teaching you how to pan, we'll just use some of the dirt from the river bed."

Her lips pursed as she nodded, her concentration shifting from him to the river. Luckily. The last time he'd kissed her, she'd responded. Their attraction to each other was hard to ignore. But she resisted it. Resisted the pull between them.

If she didn't want anything to do with him in that way, fine. He had never forced his attentions on a woman, and he certainly wouldn't force anything on Clara. In fact, he'd shoot any man who attempted such a thing.

He scowled at the river before he realized what he was doing and cursed silently. He was in deeper than he thought if just imagining another man kissing her got to him.

It was better that she wanted nothing to do with him. The town would have a fit if they were together. But even as he thought that, he knew none of it mattered. If Clara wanted him, he'd be a damned fool to turn her away.

He wasn't a fool.

"What is it?" she asked.

"Huh?"

She cocked a hip, and her knee popped out beneath the layers of pinned up skirt. *Mercy.* She had legs men worshiped.

"Why are you scowling? Did I do something wrong already?" She frowned, looking down at her empty pan.

He chuckled at her confusion. Hell, *he* was confused. The whole situation was baffling because he was attracted to her but refused to do anything about it. "No. Sorry. Thinking of something else. Start by scooping up silt in your pan from the riverbed. Don't worry about getting it too full."

She bent over, and her skirt rode a little higher in the back, but he kept his eyes on her face. He should be sainted for such self control.

She came back up with a half-full pan. "That's good. Now, lean back down and add some fresh water to the pan and shake it back and forth."

She dipped the pan in and gently swirled the water. "Like this?"

"You need to do it harder, faster." He closed his

eyes. Lord, have mercy. If he could just get through this lesson and only think of panning, he'd be lucky. "Essentially, what you're doing is trying to get rid of the pebbles and silt. As you shake, the lighter stuff, the stuff that you don't want, will rise to the top, allowing the gold to fall to the bottom of the pan."

She shook harder and some silt clouded the water, but it still wasn't enough.

Steeling himself, he placed his hands over hers, relishing how warm she was, how sweet she smelled, but refused to allow himself to do anything else. He shook the pan firmly through her hands, showing her the quick shakes needed to produce the correct results. "You'll want to begin like that. Once you've gotten rid of most of the silt, you'll do it softer."

He stepped back and watched her copy the motion and nodded his approval. She learned quickly. "Good. Now, as the water gets murky, you'll want to empty it and get fresh water."

He demonstrated how to get rid of it and refill without losing the heavier material.

She followed his instructions exactly. Refill, shake, rinse. Refill, shake, rinse. She did this until little remained in her pan. She swirled the final pieces across the bottom, and he leaned over to see the results.

"There." He pointed to a small nugget. Nothing like the size he'd dug out of his mine, but it was still gold. "That's gold."

She gasped. "It is?" She scoured the pan with her gaze. "What about that?"

He eyed the piece she pointed to and shook his

head. "No. That's iron."

"This?"

She pointed out another piece, and he grinned. "Gold."

"Yes! I did it." The smile that flashed to her face robbed him of breath. "I found gold." She did a little dance in the river before twirling. "Thank you. I couldn't have done this without you."

He chuckled at her joy. She was so beautiful it actually ached to look at her. The need to hold her, to kiss her, overwhelmed him.

She twirled again holding the pan in the air a moment before her foot caught on a rock.

His hand reached out to steady her as she teetered, but it was too late. Unfortunately, his legs hadn't been braced to catch her, and they both fell into the stream, he on top of her.

"Oomph!"

Horrified, he scrambled, pulling her up until the water was chest high with her arms braced behind her. "Are you hurt? Are you all right?"

She snorted with her head down, and he was worried she had water in her lungs. Reaching behind her, he whacked her back gently, until her snorts turned into laughter.

His hand stilled on her back as wet, merry-filled eyes looked into his. Giggles escaped her lips, and the sound of pure joy pulled chuckles from his own lips. "I take it you're not choking."

Peels of laughter escaped her a moment before she looped her arm around his neck and pulled his lips down to hers for a quick kiss.

His body went rigid when she broke the

connection, but she didn't let go, just continued to smile into his eyes.

"What was that for?" he asked huskily.

"I wanted to thank you."

"For what?" Whatever it was, he'd do it over and over again if she would just press her lips to his again.

"For helping me find gold. For making me laugh." She giggled. "For trying to stop me from drowning."

His head ducked as he thought of the way he'd pounded her back. It all seemed so ridiculous now. "I do what I can."

"Thank you, Sawyer."

He shivered, hearing his name on her lips. Damn, it felt good. *Too* good. "You're welcome."

He should pull away. He knew that. But he didn't want to. His body caged hers in the water, rising above her in a way that felt both protective and dominating. Having her beneath him, even with layers of clothes and water between them, felt good. He wasn't ready to give that up.

Apparently, neither was she.

She tugged on his neck again, but this time, he lowered his head slowly, allowing the tension between them to build. The trickling stream turned to a full blown rush of sound as his heart accelerated.

One more kiss would be enough. One more taste. He wouldn't take anything else from her. But he needed this.

He lowered his head, thrilled when she closed her eyes on a shiver. When his lips touched hers again, it was his turn to shake.

He took her slowly, gently, reveling in her taste as the sun heated his back.

She murmured something between the soft grazes of lips, moaning when he kissed her deeper.

She tasted like heaven. Like the first strike of gold. Like spring after a bitterly cold winter.

Like home.

Like mine.

The possessive thought startled him enough to pull from her lips. He searched her hazy eyes, her rosy lips.

His.

"Sawyer?" she asked, confusion filling her eyes. "Are you all right?"

"Yeah." He said it a bit too quickly.

He jumped up and reached down for her, taking her hands quickly before pulling her up. She allowed her body to overshoot, and she fell into him.

He hissed out a breath as the feel of her soaking form pressed against him, the delicious heat of her skin burrowing through his wet clothes.

If he didn't get away from her right now, this very second, he was going to do something he'd regret. "We should, ah, probably get out of these wet clothes." He cursed. "I mean separate. At the house. Back at the house in different rooms."

Could he sound any more idiotic?

She smiled, clearly amused by his asinine response. "Probably wise."

She looked up at the sky, closing her eyes while taking a deep breath.

He almost swallowed his tongue. How was such beauty possible? He'd never seen any woman to rival her, and he knew he never would.

"Can we come back soon?"

He was starting to realize that he'd take her anywhere she wanted. "We can come whenever you like. I still need to show you how to mine too."

"Tomorrow?"

He nodded, sealing his fate.

Chapter Ten

Clara hummed as she worked in the garden. Sylvia forbade any of the women to help around the house, insisting that such things were her job. But that didn't sit well with Clara.

Frankly, the inactivity was driving her crazy. She would be with Sawyer in a few hours, learning to mine, but until then, she had nothing else to do.

Sylvia would just have to deal with finding the vegetable garden weeded. And weeded well.

A snort sounded from behind her. "You're going to get in trouble for that."

Clara turned, dirt in hand as she eyed a snickering Belle lingering in the doorway. "Only if *someone* tells her who did it."

"My lips are sealed."

Belle marched over to Clara's side. It wasn't graceful, but she didn't look clumsy either. Clara realized it was just the way the woman walked. "Did you need something?"

Belle shuffled her walking boots. "I just thought you should know. Some of the women are inside. *Talking.*" She glanced back at the house pointedly.

Warning bells went off. *What now?* "About what exactly?"

"Well, some of them are upset." She waited, but must have realized that Clara wasn't catching on. "Upset about you and Sheriff Morrison."

Sheriff Morrison? "What could they possibly be upset about?"

Belle squared her shoulders, gearing up to break the news. "Sadie saw you kiss the sheriff in the river. She told Willow. Unfortunately, Willow told the rest of us."

Clara laughed. "That's all? Why would everyone be upset about that?"

"Violet's got everyone all worked up that you've been volunteering to learn to mine so you could spend more time with him. She made it seem like you're stealing him away from the rest of us."

"What?" Clara tossed the dirt down and rose with a strike. "That's preposterous!"

Belle held up her hands. "*I* know that. I'm on your side."

"I didn't realize that I needed to have a side."

"You don't." Belle's shoulders fell. "I'm sorry."

Clara shook her head hard as she ground her teeth. "You don't need to be. This whole thing is ridiculous."

She took a step toward the house in righteous fury before Belle reached out to stop her. "What are you going to do?"

"Straighten this out. You coming?" Clara arched

a brow sharply before brushing past her friend and into the house.

Straight into mutiny.

All eyes turned to her when she entered, and Belle stepped around her to join the others.

Clara met Sadie's eyes before the woman mouthed *I'm sorry*.

The apology and the upset in Sadie's eyes alleviated a little of her wrath. At least she hadn't meant for this fecal flurry to start. It took some of the sting away.

"Belle told me we have a problem. Although I'm afraid I'm not quite sure if I believe her. She informed me that Sadie saw me kissing the sheriff, and that some of you are upset by that. Is this true?"

Willow stepped forward. "You're damn right we're upset. You're supposed to be helping us. Not stealing away a perfectly good marriage candidate."

A few murmured their agreements, but she noticed that not all agreed with Willow's sentiment. It didn't matter though. Her temper was slow to light, but when it did, it burned hotly.

She stared down the group. Willow and Violet didn't turn away, but Rosalie lowered her gaze. "Are you telling me, that I'm not allowed to find someone? That I'm not as equally deserving of love as you all?"

Violet swaggered closer and cocked a hip. "You're supposed to be helping us. Not whoring yourself out."

Olivia and Juliette gasped.

Clara's hand flew out, striking Violet's cheek before Clara even realized what she was doing. The move to violence shocked her, and her voice shook. "Don't ever call me that again. I think you've all forgotten that I am one of Ivan's mail-order brides too. I may have volunteered to help us for the good of all, but I'm certainly not a servant, and I have zero intention of waiting on the sidelines to find love. I would never begrudge any of you that. Not after what we've been through."

"Is that what you've found?" Juliette asked, her black eyes quiet, watching. "Love?"

All eyes turned to hers. Even Violet's glaring ones, but she didn't say a word against Clara after the slap. "I don't know exactly what I feel for Sawyer, but one thing I do know is that it's none your business unless I confide in you. I've been working with Sawyer to secure our finances because I'm happy to help the group. I want to help. But if any of you think I'm not doing a good enough job, you're welcome to step forward and help."

Silence echoed through the room as she turned away. She was sick of taking care of everyone. Sick of being the one to handle the tough questions. For right now, she was done. She needed to get away, to regroup and think about her next steps.

Living in such a large family hadn't prepared her to handle a confrontation with nine unmarried women. At least some of her siblings had taken her side. And while Belle, Olivia, and Sadie weren't upset with her relationship with Sawyer, they hadn't spoken up for her either.

She just hoped they all survived long enough to get married and move on.

At the moment, it didn't seem likely.

"WHEN YOU MINE, THE NUMBER one thing you should be thinking of is safety. Any number of things can happen if you aren't careful."

Sawyer began his explanation outside the cave. To his surprise, all of the women were there that sunny afternoon to learn the basics of how to find gold. All except Banshee. But when he'd asked after her whereabouts, the women looked everywhere but him, and someone mentioned that she was busy with a household chore.

He didn't understand women all that well, but he knew trouble. And this reeked of it. But he wasn't too concerned. If it only had to do with Banshee and her temper, he was surprised the ladies hadn't gotten into arguments more often. If it got out of hand, he would step in and ask Clara for more information. Until then, he was happy to leave domestic issues to the ladies.

He frowned as he glanced at Clara. She'd hardly looked at him. Perhaps there was something more going on.

Juliette raised her hand before speaking. "I know you've already told us where the richest deposits are most likely to be found, but could you explain your reasoning? I'd like to understand why."

Willow rolled her eyes, but he ignored her. Juliette was book smart with an intellect that exceeded most men in his acquaintance. If she wanted to know the details of gold hunting, he was happy to share.

He spent the next thirty minutes explaining the basics of mining and best uses of the tools laid out on the ground. Questions were peppered throughout the lesson, but none were from Clara. In fact, she'd done her best to remain quiet and distant since they started.

"Why don't you all familiarize yourselves with the tools? It's better to examine them and practice wielding them outside rather than when you're in the cave when light is scarce."

The women chatted as they picked up brushes, axes, metal rods, and hammers. The tools of his former life. Tools that he thought he'd never have need of again.

His eyes finally connected with Clara's. "Clara, can I have a word with you?"

She glanced around uneasy at the group before nodding.

He took her arm and led her behind a tree so the others wouldn't stare. "What's wrong?"

She extracted her arm from his grip. "Nothing."

"Don't give me that." He pointed at the group beyond the greenery. "There's something going on with you all, and I want to know what it is. At first I thought Banshee might be causing more problems, but I can tell it's something more."

Clara's eyes widened.

"What?" he asked.

She swallowed hard, pressing her lips together, but an amused gasp slipped out. "Who—" gasp "—is Banshee?"

"Violet." His eyes narrowed when she chuckled softly, but his stern look didn't last long. He finally chuckled with her and ran a hand through his hair. She was driving him crazy. "Probably not the most flattering name."

"But fitting," she agreed.

He loved seeing a smile on her face. Even if it was a hesitant one. He hadn't realized how much he needed that until this moment. During his lecture, when she'd been distant and quiet, it disturbed him. He didn't want her removed emotionally from him. He wanted her smiles, her laughter, her sweetness. And he was selfish enough to admit that he wanted them all to himself.

All traces of amusement slowly faded from her face, and it hurt his heart.

He leaned a hand against the tree, caging her with his body.

She looked toward the ground, and he spotted a cowlick in her hair, peeking through the simple pink ribbon falling out of her dark curls. "Tell me what's bothering you."

"It's nothing."

"We both know it's not."

She sighed and finally looked up at him. "There was an argument today."

"About?"

"Someone saw us panning for gold."

"And that's a problem because…?"

She swallowed. "Because they saw us in the river after too."

"I see." He did. Kind of. Why would their kiss cause such contention? Did they look down on her for it? A protective surge swelled in his chest. "Are they giving you a hard time about it?"

She nodded.

He notched her chin up, needed her to see the sincerity in his eyes. "I hope you know how much I respect you. I would never ask for anything more than a kiss."

"I know that. Of course."

"Do I need to tell the other's that?"

Her brows furrowed. "I don't see why that would help."

Now he felt uncomfortable. "So they'd know that you're not a woman of ill-repute."

Her mouth fell open.

He rushed to quickly say, "I know that. I just want them to know that too."

"Besides a few hateful comments from Violet, I'm fairly certain that no one thinks that."

Now it was his turn to be confused. "Then why are they giving you a hard time?"

"Honestly?" He nodded so she knew he really wanted to know. "They're upset because they feel like I've stolen you away from them."

"Stolen?" What was she talking about?

"They think I volunteered to help learn how to find gold so I could spend more time with you. Become closer to you."

He didn't comment on her blush. No doubt the whole thing embarrassed her. Hell, if he wasn't so frustrated, he probably would be as well. "That's ridiculous. Any one of them could've come to me for help. I would've showed them all how to mine..." Realization dawned. "Is that why they're all here today?"

She nodded with round, solemn eyes.

He looked away and swore.

At her gasp, he turned back to her and apologized before saying, "I want you to know that I didn't kiss you because you were the only one available to me. I kissed you because I'm attracted to you. Only," he continued when she was about to speak, "you. When I had all of you gathered together in the hotel lobby, I had no interest in any of Ivan's brides. None, until you walked in the room."

She didn't say anything, just seemed to absorb his words.

He raked another hand through his hair, trying to come up with something to set her at ease. "I didn't plan for any of this to happen. The kiss in the river just happened. I can't say it won't again."

A slow smile reached her eyes. "You can't?"

He shook his head slowly, mesmerized by the small glow in her eyes. The light he'd put there. "No. I can't."

He leaned in to brush a soft kiss across her lips. A kiss full of promises.

The feather touch caused his heart to beat harder, but he didn't deepen the connection.

When he pulled back, her eyes fluttered open. "What's between us has nothing to do with those women over there."

"What's between us?" she asked quietly.

That was the same question he'd been asking himself since their kiss yesterday. He'd brushed off their moment in the kitchen on the day of the picnic as a one time thing, but when they'd been at the river, there'd been something more.

He'd never imagined himself married or in love or anything else he so often saw happen to other people. It's not that he was opposed to it exactly, he'd just never desired those things for himself. Whatever was happening between them was new. "I don't know. Maybe something. Maybe nothing. But whatever this is or isn't, is between us and no one else. All right?"

She nodded. "All right."

"Good." He smiled. "Now, why don't we head back and bring the group into the mine? I have a feeling this will either kill me or amuse me greatly."

She laughed as she led him back to the women.

Chapter Eleven

H eaven save them all from lady miners.

If it was the last thing Sawyer did, he would find someone to take over the mining operation at Ivan's claim. Today.

He never wanted to go through a mining lesson with that particular group of women again. Aria almost lost a finger, Willow lamented the stains on her gowns more than she wielded her tools, and Juliette almost caused a cave-in due to her desire to experiment.

Heaven above, he knew they meant well, but he would not do that again. If he had to crawl on his belly and beg someone to take them off his hands, he would.

He'd promised Clara he'd help, and that's exactly what he was doing. He was helping by getting them a hired hand.

The second he stepped onto the boardwalk outside the saloon, Katie, one of the girls who worked there, flew out of the door and into his arms.

"Katie?"

"Shhh." She begged, yanking his arms around her waist. "Play along."

"With what?"

When a man who looked meaner than a pissed off bull charged out the doors, Katie fused her lips to his.

Wrong! Shock bolted through him. He pulled away from her after his surprise wore off.

She stroked his cheek, and it took all of his willpower not to remove her hand. "Come on darlin' I'm just wantin' a taste before the main course," she said.

Gah. He didn't need to be a genius to see why Katie was putting on such a show. The man who'd chased after her slinked back inside after the display, and she sagged against him.

"I'm sorry," she whispered. Her embarrassment and shame were evident. "If he didn't think I was with someone else, he'd have pulled me into a room for sure. He has a mean look in his eye."

She'd read the man right. Sawyer could feel the man's cruel streak. "It's all right. You know if something ever happens, you can come to me. No one is allowed to hurt you."

She nodded hard. "I do."

"Good." He put more distance between them. "I'm here for Ronan. Have you seen him?"

"He's inside. It's one of those nights."

"I'll remember that," he said. *Those* nights, where men were drunk and volatile, didn't happen too often anymore now that they were trying to establish themselves. But they were still men. And liquor and poker was still a favorite past time.

He entered the saloon and scanned the dim surroundings. It was late afternoon, and there was already a crowd gathering at the bar and around a boisterous poker game played in the middle of the room.

Exactly what he was looking for.

He'd come up with a list of possible men to work the mine. Some were better than others. None great.

Except one.

He stepped toward the poker table and watched as Ronan Briggs pushed a tumbling stack of bills and coins into the center of the table without blinking.

The man sitting adjacent to him sweated as he looked between his cards and the steely expression on his opponent's face.

Stone.

That's what Ronan looked like. He was a fierce player. Both in cards and in life. He never did anything half measure. He won it all, or lost it all. Fortunately for him, he'd mined a fortune and could cover any loss he pleased.

"Well?" Ronan asked the other player. "Are you in or out?"

"Aww, Ronan. You can't just throw it all in the pot," the man whined, looking at his cards one last time.

Ronan's face didn't soften.

The man sighed and laid his cards down. "I'm out."

Not even a smirk lifted Ronan's lips, and Sawyer wondered if the man ever felt joy in his winnings. He certainly never looked like it.

Ronan bundled up his prize before his opponent reached out and grabbed his hand. "Hey, you can't just up and leave. I'm needing a chance to win it back."

Ronan glared, and Sawyer took a step forward. This could turn out badly.

"Take your hand off me," Ronan said, punctuating each word.

The other man's eyes widened, and he released Ronan as if scalded.

"I'm doing you a favor by leaving. If I stay, you'll only lose more."

Truer words had never been spoken. By the look of Ronan's pile, he was on a winning streak. He could've taken the man's home, if he'd a mind to.

The man grumbled, and Ronan turned to leave.

The moment his back was turned, the loser pulled a gun.

Before Sawyer could pull his weapon free, Ronan's was up and pointed at the man he'd just cleaned out. "Don't do anything stupid."

The man's hand shook, and he glanced around at the frozen room, the bystanders holding their breath as they watched the tense scene unfold.

Sawyer rocked back onto his heels. "If either of you shoots, I'll have to arrest you. Don't make me do that," Sawyer said casually, hoping to diffuse the situation.

Ronan didn't move a muscle. "No one's shooting anybody, are they?" He cocked his head an inch.

The loser's eyes darted around again before he lowered his weapon. "Nuh uh."

Ronan didn't waste any more time on words. He holstered his weapon and pushed his way out of the stifling room.

Sawyer followed him, cursing under his breath. You'd think there'd be a better time to approach him, but there wasn't. Ronan's moods were mercurial.

"Ronan, hold on a minute."

Ronan didn't look up from saddling his gelding. "I'm not causing trouble, sheriff."

"I know. I wanted to talk to you about something else." Sawyer stopped on the boardwalk and took the man's silence as permission to continue talking. "I have a job for you."

"Yeah? Not interested."

The man hadn't even glanced over his shoulder before turning him down. "Don't you want to hear what it is? Aren't you curious?"

"Nope and nope."

Finished with his task, Ronan finally turned around to face Sawyer. Wearing black from head to toe, Ronan folded his arms and leaned casually against the hitching post. At least he appeared casual. As he'd just demonstrated in the saloon, he could be as quickly vicious as a mountain lion after a long winter.

He'd never seen Ronan soften toward anyone. The only person he seemed to have any sort of relationship with was Asher Walker, the mountain man who'd found his fiancé dead after she'd been kidnapped. And even then, Ronan hated him. But it was some semblance of feeling.

Right now, Ronan didn't look like he was going to budge. "If that's all, Sheriff, I need to get going." He turned around and gripped his saddle to mount.

Sawyer sighed. He hated to ever call in favors. He preferred that men do as he asked instead of being forced into it, but it looked like he didn't have a choice. "Bannack."

Ronan let out a foul curse and whipped around. "What did you say?"

Sawyer took a step closer. "Bannack."

Ronan's hands closed into fists. "What do you want?"

"You've heard about Ivan's brides?"

"I'm not deaf."

"They need help working the mine."

"And you want me to do it for them?"

"You're the best option."

Ronan laughed harshly. "I'm your only option."

While Sawyer had a few others in mind, he knew Ronan was right. There was no other man he trusted to work the mine honestly and leave the women alone. "Will you do it?"

"How long?"

"Depends." Sawyer rubbed his jaw. "The women should marry rather quickly. Their husbands will probably want to take over."

"What's my cut?"

"Ten percent."

"Twenty."

"Fifteen."

"Done." A slow smile spread on Sawyer's face.

Ronan shrugged and climbed on his horse. "After

I do this, we're even."

"Agreed."

Ronan motioned his horse into a trot, and Sawyer watched him as he kicked up dust. Sawyer had never thought twice of the debt Ronan owed him. When you save a man's life, you don't expect anything in return. But Sawyer knew Ronan didn't see it like that.

They'd first met in Bannack, years after the gold rush's peak, and most of the gold had already been found. Sawyer and his brother had just been in the right place at the right time to save Ronan's life after robbers had shot him and left him for dead.

And at the moment, Sawyer was grateful.

Ronan would eliminate this problem.

Now, all he needed to do was to keep the women safe. That was, if they didn't kill themselves first.

RESOLUTE, CLARA SADDLED A HORSE and rode to town. The air was crisp and fresh regardless that it was nearly dinner time. Birds sung, bees buzzed, and animals seemed content to frolic in the open meadows.

She understood their happiness. For the first time in years, she felt peace, excitement, contentment.

She had come to marry Ivan, and it had all fallen through only to give her something even better in return. She was still upset with the women, but she was needed here. And while that filled her heart with a sense of fulfillment, it wasn't everything to her.

She had Sawyer.

She'd thought she had to hold herself back from him because it would take away from her duty to the other women, but that wasn't true. She didn't need to only care for one or the other. She could care for everyone. Her heart was big enough to let them all in. He'd shown her that at the mine.

She pulled into town and dismounted from her horse in front of the jail, but after a quick look inside, found that it was empty.

Where else would Sawyer be?

She strode down the boardwalk, looking through windows as she passed. While she felt safe enough in town, she remembered what had happened the last time she was here, and she wasn't going to take any chances.

He had to be here somewhere.

But as she passed the barber shop, blacksmith, mercantile, and hotel, the options for where he was were lessening.

She gazed up at the saloon and spotted him outside the doors. Relief swept through her. She'd found him, and at least she wouldn't have to venture inside that male domain to locate him.

She raised her hand, about to call out to him when a scantily dressed woman rushed through the doors and into Sawyer's arms, planting a kiss on his lips.

Clara's feet planted like lead in the ground.

The kiss didn't last long, and Sawyer pulled away, but he didn't immediately release the woman.

Tears filled Clara's eyes, but she refused to let them fall.

How could she have been so stupid?

Instead of confronting him, she turned away and walked back to her horse, her body feeling old and fragile. She didn't know what to think or how to feel.

Hurt. That was definitely there. And anger. But she also felt shame and plenty of self-loathing. She only had herself to blame. She'd allowed her feelings for Sawyer to grow to out of control proportions without getting to know him first. She'd leapt ahead without looking, and cared for him regardless of what she felt she owed the other women.

At the mine, he'd told her that there might be nothing between them. Why had she ignored that and allowed herself to continue feeling more for him?

Had she really stood up to the other woman, defending her relationship with Sawyer just this morning?

And now this.

She was a fool. And she would be twice the fool if she kept her heart open to him. A man who dallies with other women wasn't worth her time. She knew that. Believed that.

No matter how much she cared for Sawyer, she couldn't do this, wouldn't allow him to trample over her heart and be unfaithful to her. If he behaved this way now, how would he act if things got more serious between them? If they married?

Her gut clenched at the thought, and she mounted her horse. Although how she managed it when her heart splintered in her chest was beyond her.

She'd known she cared for Sawyer. She just hadn't known she was in love with him.

Chapter Twelve

———✦———

"**W**hat do you mean Clara's in the mine?" Sawyer asked Belle from the porch when she blocked him from entering.

"I thought I was clear. We've no need of your help. We're working the mine ourselves."

Sawyer had no words. Literally. He alternated between wanting to threaten, throw up his hands, shake the woman, and chase down Clara. The latter won. "We'll see about that."

He launched on his horse and didn't slow his mount until he was at the mine. "Clara! Clara!" He yelled from outside but doubted she was in the front and able to hear him.

He'd have to go in after her.

Cursing, he tied his horse to a post, next to hers, and strode over to the supplies laid out. He lit an enclosed lamp, swearing again when the match singed his finger.

That woman would answer for this. Didn't she

know how dangerous mining alone was? He'd explained that to her, to them all. That even if they decided to work, they should have someone with them at all times.

Besides that, after the lesson, he'd told her he'd find someone to work it. What had possessed her to do such a thing? To jeopardize her safety?

"Clara?" He called out and heard her voice echoing a response. He followed the sound until he found her, her chin notched up, proud, regardless of the cute dirt patches smeared on her cheek and clothes.

"What are you doing here?" she asked.

"What am *I* doing here? What are you doing here? Alone? I told you it wasn't safe. What possessed you to take such a risk?"

It took everything in his willpower to keep his hands to himself instead of wrapping them around her body and hauling her out of there.

Her lips firmed. "What I do is no longer your concern, Sheriff."

His mouth dropped open. "Sheriff? We're back to that? What on earth is going on?"

"Nothing." She shrugged. "I just realized that the only people the women and I can count on are ourselves."

He didn't recognize the combative woman in front of him. Not more than twenty-four hours earlier, everything was great. They'd had a plan. He'd even gotten Ronan to help. "What happened? Why are you doing this?"

"I was in town yesterday afternoon. I saw you."

"All right." He shook his head, still not

understanding. "If you did, why didn't you come up to me? I would've helped you with whatever you needed."

She laughed humorlessly. "Oh. I have no doubt of that. You seem to help all women equally."

He slowly nodded at the truth of her words even if they felt like a trap. "I do. All women deserve help."

"And is that what you were doing with that woman from the saloon?" She lashed out, her eyes blazing. "Were you helping her when you kissed her?"

"What?" Sawyer reeled. "What are you talking about? I didn't kiss—" But then he remembered the incident with Katie.

"You know what I'm talking about." She crossed her arms, and he couldn't help but feel a surge of attraction. But he didn't think she'd appreciate him scooping her in his arms.

"It's true, Katie did kiss me."

"Ha!" She flung her arms in the air. "You admit it."

"Now, hold on." When her arm flailed toward him, he gripped her hand to stop the slap, but he held her gently. "Katie did kiss me, but it wasn't what it looked like, nor did I want her to."

"Sure. You were really fighting her off," she scoffed.

He reached for her upper arms and pulled her closer. She didn't resist, but her body didn't meld into his like he'd come to savor. "She needed my protection from another man." When she tried to pull away, he held her close and forced her gaze to meet his. "A *man* who would've hurt her had she not pretended that she was already taken that night."

She stilled, really listening to him so he continued, "I'm not involved with Katie, and I never have been. I've never had a relationship with any of the women in town. But they all know that I'll help them. I don't care if they're a rancher's wife, prostitute, or... mail-order bride."

Silence filled the tunnel a moment before she tugged her hand from his. "Why should I believe you?" she asked softly.

He didn't take offense. They didn't know enough about each other to trust blindly. But he wanted to know her. For her to know him. "Because you can. Ask anyone else around here, and they'll tell you the same thing."

Her chin trembled before she turned away. Picking up her ax, she struck into the rock, dislodging chunks. "I want to. But it's hard."

"Don't you mean scary? Trusting another is terrifying because it leaves you vulnerable."

She finally nodded but didn't look back at him. "I'm not used to depending on others."

"Not even your family?"

"No. They were there, but I always had to take care of myself and usually several of my siblings. That's just how it was." She shrugged. "I didn't mind it. But it makes opening myself up to others difficult. I don't know if I can."

"You won't know until you try."

Her shoulders sagged, the ax falling low as his words penetrated. He wanted to go to her, to take her into his arms. But this had to be her choice. She had to choose to let him into her life. She had to choose to trust him. He could never force her to do so, and even if he tried and succeeded, he knew it'd never last.

As if making up her mind, she nodded, hoisting the ax once more and jamming it into the wall a final time.

A smile crept to his lips, but a sharp cracking sound had the hairs on his neck rising.

The mine boomed.

Eyes wild, he leaped forward and covered Clara's body with his own.

A cloud of dust and rocks roared over them, slicing at his skin as the tunnel behind them collapsed. Clara screamed beneath him, and he prayed the collapse was localized and wouldn't set off a chain reaction throughout the whole mine.

Stones continued to trickle from the ceiling, but after a few moments, he dared a look up, his breath heaving through gritty air.

Fortunately, the lamp hadn't gone out, and he was able to see a little in the thick, dusty air. This tunnel was holding.

For now.

He looked down at Clara, tucked in a ball beneath him. "Are you all right?"

"I'm not hurt." She coughed.

He stood, wincing at a particularly deep cut on his arm. The fresh blood trickling down his arm was a stark contrast to his grubby clothes.

He helped her stand. She looked around the tunnel with wide, scared eyes. He didn't blame her. Cave-ins ended in death—if you were lucky. The bastards who were stuck in mines, surviving catastrophes only to suffocate or starve to death, they were the truly unlucky ones.

"Are we going to die?"

His lips firmed. "I won't lie to you. It'll be hard." Before she could panic he added, "But I'm going to do everything in my power to get us out of here." He shook her so her glassy eyes would focus on his. "Do you understand me? I'm going to get us out of here."

He would. He didn't care what he had to do. He'd go to hell and back if it would save her life. He hadn't been able to save his parents, but he'd made it his life to protect others. And he would save hers.

"How will we get out?" Hope lit in her eyes. "The others know I'm here. If I'm not home by dark, they'll come looking for me."

"They know I'm here too."

"They do?"

"I stopped by the house first to find you."

"Oh." She looked around again, and her eyes filled. "You came here for me." She nodded, and a tear slid down her cheek. "You're in here because of me. Because I was stupid."

"No." He shook his head firmly. "You weren't stupid. You were mad. Hell, I would've been furious had I seen you kissing another man. For any reason."

A watery smile crossed her lips. "You don't need to be nice to me. I might've killed you."

Unable to see her sad, he leaned in quick, kissing her hard, and then took her hand. "We're not dead yet. Come on." He grabbed the lamp before tugging her deeper into the tunnel.

"Where are we going? This can't be safe." She lifted her skirt hem before tripping over a rock.

He eyed the dragging fabric, all sorts of things could happen to the yards of material in a mine. It could catch fire, cover rocks so she'd lose her footing, or even snag something it shouldn't. "Why don't you tie your skirts up like you did at the river? It could prevent something bad from happening."

"You mean," she said before pushing the fabric through her legs and bringing it around to tie in front, "like a cave-in? Done that. And my skirts didn't cause that."

"Very funny."

"You really think you can get us out of here?"

"Yes."

"How?"

He looked down the tunnel. "Ivan might've been crazy, but he wasn't stupid. He knew about the dangers of mining as well as anyone. He'd have had another entrance into the mine."

She gasped, then coughed. "Really? You think?"

"Yes." But he couldn't let her rest all of her hopes on something hypothetical. "But even if he didn't, we'll find a way out."

She nodded before he took her hand again and walked down the tunnel.

Rocks occasionally fell from the ceiling, but it looked like the structure would hold. Hopefully.

After ten minutes of silence, Clara spoke. "Why did you come? To find me," she added.

"I came to tell you that I found someone to work for you." He glanced back at her a moment before continuing on.

"You did?" She sounded relieved. "I'm glad. After this, I'm never setting foot in a mine again."

He chuckled. He couldn't say he relished the thought of heading back in any time soon either.

"Who is he?"

"His name is Ronan Briggs. He's…" What could he say? *He's a gambler that loses big sometimes. He's a recluse who's almost more gunfighter than miner. I saved his life.* "He knows how to mine."

She snorted, but he couldn't tell if it was from the dust or her response to his statement. "Why isn't he working his own then?"

"His paid out already."

"Oh." She seemed to mull that information over. "That's nice of him to do it then."

He winced. He couldn't have Clara thinking Ronan was doing it out of the kindness of his heart. "I wouldn't say he was being nice, exactly."

She stopped their progress and forced him to meet her eyes in the dimly lit passage.

"What do you mean he wasn't being nice? He didn't want to do it?"

"Not exactly," he hedged.

"Well, what exactly did he or didn't he want to do?"

"He didn't want to help."

She frowned. "And you convinced him? How?"

"I called in a debt."

Her mouth fell open. "A debt? Can't we find someone else who's a little more willing? I think with the right person, they'd be motivated just by the money."

Sawyer shook his head vehemently. This is where she was wrong. Dead wrong. "That is not the kind of person you want working for you."

"The motivated kind?"

"The kind who will rob you blind."

She seemed to mull that over. "I see."

He nodded, grateful that she did. "A lot of men would take advantage of the situation."

"And you don't think Ronan will?"

"No." That was something he'd bet his life on. "He has his downsides, but he's always been honest, and he has enough money of his own that he won't need to take yours."

"Okay. If you say he's the right choice, I trust you."

It was amazing how just a few words could change you inside. Hearing her say she believed in him, that she was putting something so important in his hands, filled him with pride.

She made him feel strong. "Thank you."

About ten minutes later, they smelled fresh air. Their steps picked up speed until they flew out of the dank mine and into twilight.

Sucking in rough breaths of air, he pulled her into his arms and just held her.

Tight.

Fitted.

Right.

Her body melted into his until they were almost one.

Her chest heaved in tandem with his as grateful lungs pulled in clean air. As their hearts filled with relief.

They were alive. They were unharmed. They'd survived.

Together.

"Are you all right?" he asked, unwilling to release her even an inch to check for himself.

Her chin nodded against his throat as she nuzzled there. "Yes. A bit dirty, but fine."

He chuckled, somehow able to find humor in the situation only moments after they'd freed themselves. "You'll recover from that."

They held each other in silence a moment longer. This could've ended so differently. He recognized that. And for the first time, allowed himself to fully feel the after effects of what had just happened.

He held her a little tighter, only loosening his grip when she squirmed.

"Sorry."

"It's okay." She leaned back to look into his eyes. "We really are okay."

He reached up and held the hand she'd lifted to his cheek. He pressed it more firmly against him a moment before turning his head and kissing it. "We should get you home. The others will be worried."

She nodded.

But that's not what he wanted to do. He wanted to cart her away, take her somewhere where they could be together. Where he could fill himself on her sweetness, her scent.

He wanted to be with her. Alone.

After coming so close to losing her, he realized one very large thing.

He loved her.

He always thought love would knock him over the head like a mine blast, but it hadn't. It had come on gradually, slowly pulling him in like thick, sticky molasses.

And he wanted to gorge himself on it.

She was everything he'd hoped for in a woman. Not that he'd planned on having one. Quite the opposite. The life of a sheriff was dangerous, and he would never purposefully tie himself to a woman who could be hurt from his line of work.

But he never had a choice. Not from the moment he'd laid eyes on her.

Now, all he had to do was convince her that out of all the men in town, he was the one she wanted.

Chapter Thirteen

Sawyer wasn't thrilled to go back up to the mine the next day, but it was best if Ronan started working right away. The sooner he pulled out gold, the better.

Sawyer had told Ronan about the cave-in, and they'd both agreed that determining the mine's state and adding additional supports for safety were the first things to be done.

Arriving at the mine, they dismounted and tied their horses to the post.

"If the entrance isn't salvageable, we'll need to make sure there's two exits. I don't want you to take any chances," Sawyer said.

Ronan grunted. "Believe me. I won't." He patted his mount and fed him something from his pocket before giving Sawyer his full attention.

The way Ronan cared for his animal spoke more about who he was as a person than anything Sawyer had heard about him. His gelding was meticulously groomed and had no marks on its flanks. And Sawyer had heard the man offer praise to his animal under his breath on more than one occasion.

If Sawyer had to guess, Ronan wasn't as big and bad as his reputation suggested. He certainly hadn't killed anyone since he'd known him. Although he was quick to draw his weapon. Sawyer could hardly blame him there, though.

More often than not, people drew against him. Couldn't condemn a man for self-defense.

They approached the front of the mine, and Ronan whistled at the mess. "Doesn't look good."

Sawyer frowned, kicking a small rock to the side as he got closer to the pile of boulders at the mouth. "No it doesn't."

Ronan nodded toward the mining supplies. Many of the lanterns were broken and several of the pick axes and sledge hammers were damaged. "Don't look like we'll be able to reuse a lot of that."

The tools wouldn't be a problem to replace. But damn it. What had caused such an accident? He'd replayed the moment before the cave-in over and over in his mind the night before, and none of it made any sense. From what he could tell, Clara hadn't wedged the ax in any deeper than normal. There weren't any open flames, and she hadn't hit any of the beams or done anything else that would set it off. None of it made sense.

"Sawyer, you'll want to come over and see this."

Ronan stared at something on the ground on the opposite side of the plugged tunnel. "What'd you find?"

Ronan nodded to a piece of timber on the

ground. "See that?"

Sawyer stared at the cleanly cut wooden support on the ground before swearing viciously.

Ronan nodded. "Who would do this?"

That's what Sawyer wanted to know. Who would purposely cut the supports to cause a cave-in? To kill whoever was inside. Or perhaps not kill someone, but just cripple the mine? "I don't know."

"This changes things."

It did. This one piece of wood changed everything. Because what Sawyer had believed to be an accident, was actually sabotage.

And he intended to find the person who dared put Clara's life in danger.

CLARA WAS STILL SHAKEN UP the day after the cave-in. Several of the women tried to talk her into staying in bed, but she wasn't having it. "I'm fine. Really. Besides, there are things to do."

Olivia shook her head. "Absolutely not. There's nothing more important than you resting today. Everything else can wait." She pushed Clara back on the sofa in her room.

In truth, Clara had thought Olivia was too gentle to boss anyone around, but right now, she was doing a fair impression of General Custer.

"She's right," Belle agreed. "There's nothing you need to worry about today except resting."

Clara looked between the two women. "You know I'll go crazy, don't you? If I have to sit here with nothing else to do but replay the moments in that mine."

Aria pushed passed the mother hens and gripped her hand. "Clara's right. It'll be better if she has something to do."

Olivia's hands went to her waist. "Oh, all right. But nothing too strenuous."

Aria rolled her eyes. "Yes, ma'am."

"Clara? Sawyer's here," Rosalie said, hovering in the doorway as she looked over Clara like an ever-watchful nurse. "Should I tell him to come back later?"

Rosalie must have decided she looked too rough for company. But Sawyer wasn't just company. She wanted to see him. "Let him in."

"If you're sure," she said as she walked out.

Olivia started fluttering around, fluffing pillows, and straightening blankets. "Now, you mustn't overtire yourself. It could give you a setback."

A setback from what? Clara wanted to ask. It wasn't as if she'd suffered from a cold. She couldn't have a setback from a cave-in unless she was transported straight back into the mine, and she was *not* going back there. But she knew Olivia was just being kind. "I won't."

When Sawyer walked in the room, her heart skipped a beat, but what was even more interesting was that, for the first time, she felt her body relax. Truly relax. As if she hadn't felt safe until this very moment.

It was ridiculous, of course. She was perfectly safe in her room, but the feeling did make her wonder. Would she ever feel safe without him?

"How are you?" he asked, discreetly glancing

over her.

"I'm well. You? How's your arm?"

He waved that away as he perched on a seat across from her. "It'll heal."

His posture put her on alert. "Is something wrong?" His jaw clenched, and her worry flared. "Did something else happen?"

"No. Nothing else." He looked around at the women gathered there. "I have some news I wanted to let you know about. All of you."

He looked at Belle. "Could you gather the rest of the women here?"

"Of course," she said, but she looked back into the room as if she worried she'd miss something.

Clara smiled encouragingly at her to go on, but it was all for show. Something was wrong.

She wanted to cry. Why must so many things go wrong? Why couldn't any of this be easy? She was sick to death of trying to force things to work and having them all fall apart.

As others filtered into the room, the noise level increased until Clara wanted to claw at her ears. Once Belle returned with Juliette, the last of them, Clara turned back to Sawyer. "Out with it."

"Clara," Olivia reprimanded, but Clara didn't care about manners just then. If she didn't have the information out of Sawyer's mouth immediately, she would scream.

"It's all right." He smiled at Olivia. "She's been through a lot. We all have."

Sadie took a hopeful step forward. "Then, you have good news?"

He sighed and took off his hat. "No. Heaven

knows I wish I did. I have more information about the cave-in. As you all know, I've hired Ronan Briggs to work the mine. We were up there earlier, scouting it out, assessing how much damage was done during the accident."

Violet glared openly at Clara, but she didn't say anything. In truth, she felt she deserved it. If it wasn't for her stubbornness, her frustration at what she'd witnessed in town, she never would've set foot in there, and none of this would be a problem. Now, supporting themselves would be ten times harder. "And what were your findings?" She wanted to know, but in truth, she dreaded it. "How bad is the damage?"

"The good news is that it shouldn't take too long to clear out the rubble. The damage was localized to the entrance of the mine."

Relief pumped through her, and she shared a smile with Belle. Everything was going to be all right. She hadn't completely messed things up.

Her attention turned back to Sawyer. "That's good, then, right?"

He nodded slowly and the smile slid from her face. Something wasn't right. "What else?" she asked.

"The mine was rigged to collapse."

Olivia gasped. "I beg your pardon?"

"Rigged?" Belle asked.

Clara was too stunned to asked anything.

"Yes. Rigged." He looked at each of the women. "The support beams were cut in a way that with little force, they'd collapse."

Willow looked ready to murder someone. "Who

would do such a thing?"

"We don't know. What we *do* know, is that someone doesn't want the mine worked."

Clara whispered, "What are we going to do?"

Sawyer only had eyes for her. His gaze caressed her face as gently as fingertips. "We'll continue doing what we've been doing. We'll just go about it a little more cautiously."

Some of the women nodded, agreeing with Sawyer's plan. But Clara couldn't stomach that.

They'd almost died yesterday. Sawyer and she could've died in the initial collapse. Or worse, slowly withered away, praying for death, trapped in the mine. If Sawyer hadn't been able to find another exit, if their lamp had gone out, if any number of other things had happened, they wouldn't be here. They wouldn't have a chance for a future together.

She couldn't let that happen again. Not to her, him, Ronan, or anyone else that stepped foot into Ivan's mine.

Into *their* mine.

She would do whatever was required to protect it. "I refuse to just sit and wait until something else happens." She looked toward the other women. "Next time, we might not be as lucky. I'm not willing to gamble with any of our lives."

"There's nothing else we can do." Sawyer shifted as if frustrated that he couldn't hunt down the person who'd caused this. "We have no suspects. No motive. No way of knowing who's behind this or why. Until we do, we need to sit tight."

Juliette cocked her head. "Why would someone want to damage the mine?"

"So no one would go in it?" Rosalie offered.

"Doesn't make sense."

Sadie wrung her hands. "Perhaps it has nothing to do with the mine at all. Maybe the person wants to hurt us."

Sawyer shook his head. "I don't think so. There's been no talk about you leaving. From the moment you arrived, everyone wanted you here."

Theories were tossed around like candy as each person offered suggestions as to why someone would damage the mine. But what really got Clara was the motivation behind it.

What prompted someone to do something so extreme? If the women were the targets, there were much more efficient ways to kill them.

She shivered at the thought.

Damaging the mine only devalued it. And from what others had told them, it wasn't worth much to begin with.

She froze, the noise around her fading.

From what she'd been told.

What if the mine was more valuable than they'd been led to believe? What if most everyone didn't know that, and that was why the mayor gave them the mine in return for them staying? The town would never have turned it over if there was a fortune to be had.

But if there was gold. And someone knew it…

Her gaze locked on to Sawyer. "Could someone be trying to damage the mine so we'd sell?"

"They might. But why go to all that trouble?"

"What if there was more gold in there than what we were told?"

"If there was, we'd know about it. Ivan would've mined it all."

"Would he have?" She cocked her head. "I didn't know Ivan well, but he was eccentric. Crazy. He had enough gold to do everything *he'd* wanted to do. What if he'd just left the rest in there?"

Sawyer opened his mouth to speak, but then closed it.

"If there is a fortune in there, and someone knows about it—"

"Then they'd want to take the mine," he said, shaking his head. "You might be right."

"But how would we know who the saboteur is?" Violet asked, her body strung tight. "It could be anyone."

"It could," Clara agreed. "But there's a way to flush them out. Leaking information that we've hit it big is the only solution. It will drive the person to desperation. With any luck, this will all be over by tomorrow night."

"No." Sawyer stepped forward as if he could physically block the thought. "It's too dangerous."

Not caring that others were around, he lifted her off the ground and shook her softly. "I almost lost you once. I'm not going to gamble with your life. We'll find the person another way."

"But not as quickly. This needs to end. Next time, it might not be my life. It could be one of theirs." Her chin notched toward the group of women who watched their exchange. "This has to happen."

His hands opened and closed over her arms as if he were trying to bring himself under control. "I can't let you do this."

"You don't have a choice." She'd be firm in this. She loved Sawyer, respected him. But she couldn't obey him right now. She wouldn't live with this hanging over her head. She wouldn't wait for the person to strike again. The next time they made a move, she'd be ready.

She would put *them* on the defensive.

She gave the other women her attention. "It's the only way if we want to end this quickly. We could do as Sawyer suggests, but we'll always be watching, wondering when and who will be targeted next. I don't want to live that way. But this is about more than just me. It's about all of us. We all need to make the choice. Together."

She felt Sawyer's unease, but was glad he remained silent. The fact that he was willing to let them all choose what to do, that he respected her enough to let them make that decision, made her love him even more.

After a vote, it was unanimous. They'd leak information tomorrow morning that a mother load had been found in Ivan's mine.

Whoever wanted the gold would come after them.

And they'd be ready.

Chapter Fourteen

Olivia volunteered to go into the mercantile the next morning and *accidentally* let it slip that they'd struck gold. In front of the town's biggest gossip.

When Sawyer had asked for someone to take over the task, he was surprised she'd stepped forward.

He liked Olivia, of course. She was a nice, fine woman. But out of all of Ivan's brides, he wouldn't have guessed she had the mettle to do it.

"People underestimate me," was the only explanation she gave.

He certainly had.

He strolled the street in front of the saloon as he had several times in the past, but he didn't feel the ease he used to. Nothing about this was easy.

Nothing was comfortable.

He should be with her. By her side. Protecting her.

But instead, he was here. Acting like everything was normal.

He hated it.

He watched the door to the mercantile and slowly began making his way down the street to be in position when Olivia exited.

Standing in the doorway, she gushed something to the owner and waved her arm enthusiastically one last time before dancing out.

He had to hand it to her, she knew how to put on a show.

"It's done," she said quietly when she reached him, then nodded brightly for any onlookers. "Sheriff, I hope you're enjoying this fine day."

He couldn't help but grin. Olivia was classically beautiful, although she couldn't compare to Clara in his mind, but what really shone was her smile.

"Absolutely. Looks like you're full of good news."

"I am!" She looked around like she'd misspoke. "But I really shouldn't say yet." Noticing the mercantile's owner's wife in the doorway, she winked.

It took all of Sawyer's strength not to laugh. He tipped his hat. "Well, I wish you well with whatever good news you have."

"Thank you!" She practically sung as she sauntered to her wagon and climbed up before snapping the lines.

Sawyer shook his head, chuckling as she drove away. He'd have to tell Clara exactly how well Olivia had played her part.

"Oh, Sheriff?" As if on cue, Mrs. Hennisy scurried down from the boardwalk and into the street to intercept him.

The gossipy woman just couldn't help herself. But in this case, Sawyer was grateful for the woman's loose tongue. "Good morning, Mrs. Hennisy. How are you?"

"Well, Sheriff. Very well." She glanced back at Olivia's retreating form. "Not as well as Miss Hardy though. Of course you know all about her astonishing news."

Sawyer's brows rose. "News? Miss Hardy didn't share anything with me."

"Oh dear." She looked down, attempting to look regretful but didn't quite succeed.

"What was her news?"

"It's a secret. I shouldn't have said anything."

He leaned forward and whispered, "I'm a civil servant, ma'am. You can trust me."

And with just that little bit of encouragement, she filled him in on all the details he'd told Olivia to share. Word of their strike would travel quickly in town. By nightfall, not a soul would be unaware of it.

As the woman wound down, the poor mayor happened to join their conversation. "Good afternoon, Sheriff. Mrs. Hennisy."

"Mayor, have you heard the news?"

Apparently, Mrs. Hennisy thought that as mayor, he'd keep the secret too. Or she just didn't care anymore. Sawyer guessed the latter.

The mayor's brows rose clear to his hairline. "Well, I'll be. I didn't think Ivan's mine would ever pay out. I reckon the whole town didn't either."

Sawyer shrugged, not wanting to outright lie to the mayor about the mine's circumstances. But Sawyer knew better than to let him in on the details of what was happening before they found the culprit. When you told one person, that person told one other, and another, until the whole town knew. That's what was happening in this case. Except by telling Mrs. Hennisy, they were speeding up the process. Her one person was actually thirty.

"I wonder what will happen to the mine once the women start marrying," Mrs. Hennisy mused. "I imagine the husbands will have a say in what happens."

The mayor nodded. "That sounds right. They would own a portion of the mine just by marrying into it."

"That first man will have a lot of power." She whistled.

There was truth in that. But Sawyer wasn't worried. He intended on marrying Clara soon. Very soon. And from what he could tell, none of the other women had formed an attachment. By marrying Clara, he would ensure that the women kept the claim's entire profit for themselves.

He'd never allow another man to come in and take it from them.

All he had to do was convince Clara to marry him. And if nothing else worked, he might just use that excuse to wrangle her to the alter.

IT WAS ALMOST ELEVEN AT night when Sawyer left the main house and headed out to the barn. He'd come by after dinner to confirm that the information they'd leaked had indeed made its way around town. He was happy to report, jokingly of course, that men were even more eager to court them now that the ladies had a fortune as well as looks.

Clara snorted as she snuffed out candles and recalled Sawyer's words As if they needed any more male attention. If they ever did hit the mother lode , she guessed there'd be similar problems. At least this way, they knew about those problems up front.

The others had gone to bed, weary from the stress of the day. Hopefully, there wouldn't be too many days like this in the future.

If they could just catch the person responsible.

She squelched one of the candles a little harder than necessary and glared at the offending bow in the wax. She'd have to fix it later. They may be pretending to have enough to never worry about wasting a candle, but that wasn't reality.

They still had to count their pennies. Their theory about why the mine was being sabotaged was just that.

A theory.

It seemed almost impossible that someone, even as crazy as Ivan, would leave large amounts of gold in there, regardless of his needs.

Footsteps sounded in the hall behind her. It had to be Sadie. She always waited to go to sleep until everyone else turned in.

She smiled at the thoughtful gesture. "I'm going

straight to bed, Sadie. You go ahead and settle in."

But when no one answered, she glanced over her shoulder toward the doorway. "Sadie?" she asked, but the hairs on her arms lifted as she saw a large shadow in the doorway. Too big to be Sadie... or any of the other women.

"If you scream, I'll shoot."

She believed him, whoever he was. With dim moonlight as the only light in the room, she was able to make out a gun in his hand but not his identity. "What do you want? Whatever it is, just take it and go."

"Exactly my intention."

He lunged toward her, and covered her mouth with a dirty bandana before she could scream. She fought against him, but she'd struggled too late.

He bound her hands behind her and turned her to face him.

Shock pulsed through her when he stepped into stronger light, the moon's rays illuminating his face.

Mayor Bracken

Why was he doing this?

Her mind filled with ideas, but none of them made sense. As if he'd heard her question, he said, "Both you and Ivan's claim are mine."

She closed her eyes in prayer. The mine. He'd rigged it to collapse.

"Why?" she asked, the word muffled by fabric.

"By taking you, marrying you, I will own a part of it. No one can stop me."

She fought against him when he tried to haul her out of the house, but only succeeded in gaining bruises on her arms and further threats of bodily harm.

She stilled when he cocked his gun.

Grunting his approval, he dug his weapon into her shoulder and forced her out the door.

❦

SAWYER MET RONAN AT THE mine early the next morning. Ronan had volunteered to stay close to it overnight in case someone tried anything, but it was quiet. Too quiet.

"Did you see anyone?" Sawyer asked. He was sure something would happened.

"Besides a few dogs in heat, things were pretty dead around here." He sounded almost disappointed.

"Someone should've come by. I would've bet money on it."

Ronan shrugged. "You would've lost it."

It was easy for Ronan to think like that. That's how he lived his life.

Sometimes you won, sometimes you lost. Except Ronan didn't seem to care either way.

"What do we do now?" the gambler asked.

Sawyer lifted his hat and ran his fingers through dirty-blond locks. "Sit tight, I guess. Not much more we can do until they make a move."

"And the women?"

"We'll continue to watch them as we have been. And you'll move forward and start clearing the mine."

Ronan shrugged again as he looked over the rubble spilling out of the entrance. "Their dime."

Then he chuckled. "I bet the mayor is dying over the news of the mine's payout."

Sawyer's instincts hummed. "Why is that?"

"Because of the debts he has. He actually tried to keep the mine for himself originally, tried to buy it cheap, but when others wanted it to be given as a bribe to the women, he caved."

"I didn't know he wanted it."

"Not a lot of people did. He tried to keep it quiet."

"How do you know about it then?"

Ronan smirked. "Let's just say I have my hand in a lot of pies around town. There isn't much that goes on without me knowing about it."

"I'll keep that in mind."

As Ronan sifted through rubble, Sawyer's mind wouldn't let go of what Ronan had said.

Sawyer had been with the mayor when he'd heard the news, and he hadn't seemed anything but genuinely surprised. He hadn't been upset, frustrated, or jealous. In fact, he'd been a little too calm. A little too collected.

As if he'd known.

Sawyer's heart hammered.

The mayor wasn't surprised about the strike because he knew about a mother lode in Ivan's mine. It was why he'd been quietly trying to buy it. It was why he'd been calm even though he was in debt and this payout was his ticket.

But if he knew there was gold, then why had he handed it over to the women? That part didn't make sense.

He didn't have solid proof, but Sawyer's

instincts screamed that Mayor Bracken was behind this.

The sound of two horses thundering their way jerked him out of his thoughts.

Belle and Olivia jerked to a halt in front of them, their eyes wild as they pulled in air.

Ronan sprung to action and pulled Olivia down from her horse before Sawyer asked, "What's wrong?"

Ronan checked Olivia for injuries. And while Sawyer had other things to think about, seeing Ronan behave so concerned over the lady gave him pause.

Belle didn't seem to notice. "Clara's missing."

"What?" Sawyer yelled. "What do you mean missing?"

"She's gone. She's not anywhere in or around the house, and none of the horses are missing."

Sawyer went cold inside. "When did you last see her?"

Olivia seemed to snap out of the shock of being manhandled by Ronan and smacked his hands away before answering. "Last night. She stayed up to make sure all the candles were extinguished. No one saw her after that."

"So she could've been missing since last night." It wasn't a question.

He was such a fool. They'd been waiting for someone to go after the mine. It never occurred to him that they'd go after one of the women.

"Why would someone take her? It can't have anything to do with the mine, could it?" Belle asked.

Sawyer shook his head, hoping the movement would calm him enough to think rationally. "I don't know. It doesn't make sense. What does taking her accomplish?"

But as he said the words, the answer hit him like lightning. "*No.*"

Ronan stepped forward. "What?"

Sawyer met the man's gaze. "I think I know who took her. And more importantly, why."

"Who?"

Sawyer closed his eyes, blocking out unwanted images of what could be happening to Clara that moment. "Mayor Bracken."

"The Mayor?" Belle asked. "But why? He's been so nice to us."

Sawyer's jaw clenched. "Because he wants the mine. And he thinks he can get his hands on it by forcing Clara to marry him."

Ronan cursed.

"We'll need Asher if we're going to find her."

Ronan's jaw clenched, but he nodded. Regardless of past feelings, Asher was the best tracker around. If anyone could find Clara, it was him.

"When do we ride?" Ronan asked.

With or without help, Sawyer *would* find her.

"Now."

Chapter Fifteen

Sawyer flew off his horse when they arrived at the small cabin deep in the mountains. Smoke lazily puffed from the chimney, signaling someone was home, but no one exited at their arrival.

"Asher!" Sawyer banged on the door, uncaring that he was out of control. "It's Sawyer Morrison, the sheriff."

Boot steps sounded inside as someone moved around. The door bolt slid to the side, and a scruffy looking man peered out. His light brown beard, tinged with red, was trimmed, but his hair was long and strands fell forward, obscuring sharp blue eyes.

Asher opened the door wider. "There's trouble," the man said, reading the situation perfectly.

"Mayor Bracken kidnapped a woman last night." Something a little wild came into Asher's eyes, but Sawyer continued, "We need you to help us track them. Will you?"

"Us?" He leaned to the side and silently studied a

stone-faced Ronan still on horseback before giving his attention back to Sawyer once again. "He agreed to come?"

"He has a personal interest here."

"Is it his woman?"

A sharp edge came into the man's voice, and Sawyer uneasily looked between them. "No. She's mine."

A little of the tension in Asher's shoulder's faded. "When was she taken?"

"We don't know for certain. But we think it was sometime last night."

Asher swore before ducking back into his house. Metal clunked together, and there was a lot of rustling inside a few moments before Asher strode out the door, hooking a small pack onto his back. "Do you know why she was taken?"

"We think he's going to try to force her to marry him."

"They'd need someone to officiate then. They could've headed in either direction out of town. There's no way to know which."

Ronan finally broke his silence. "We'll head in opposite directions. Cover the most ground."

The idea was sound. "I could head south," Sawyer suggested.

"No." Ronan firmly shook his head. "You and Asher will head south, and I'll cover the north road. It makes more sense that they'd head south and hide in a large town, but just to be safe, I'll search the small towns north of here."

When Sawyer looked to Asher for an opinion, the man tightly nodded. "I agree with Ronan.

Splitting up gives us the best opportunity to find her quickly."

"Fine." Sawyer didn't want to argue. Not when he had no idea what was the best course of action. Asher had tracked more people that Sawyer could count, and he would trust him on this. "Let's go."

They rode out quickly. Traveling back into town wasted time, but there were no shortcuts to the main roads.

As they rode down Main Street, the town bustled with even more activity than usual. Men ran back and forth between buildings and their horses in a frenzy, and Sawyer guessed that they'd heard about the kidnapping. "Damn."

When Sawyer slowed his mount, Ronan snapped, "Make it quick. We don't have time to waste."

Something had to be done to quell the posse before they hunted down the mayor. Letting those men leave town, armed with both knives and guns, would only cause Sawyer more trouble in the long run.

Sawyer nodded his head north. "There's no reason you need to stay. I'll take care of this, and then Asher and I will ride out."

"Don't take too long," Ronan warned before urging his mount on the north road. He'd still made no move to talk to Asher, but the mountain man didn't seem surprised or offended.

Moving his horse toward the crowd, Sawyer decided it was best if he stayed on his mount. The men would ask him question after question until precious time was lost.

"There's the sheriff!" One of the men called out, and a group of angry men circled him.

Someone shouted, "One of the women was taken."

"By the mayor," another called out. "We're going after them."

A chorus of agreement filled the air. This was getting out of hand.

Sawyer leaned forward in his saddle. "I need all of you to listen. I don't have much time, but I need you to cancel your hunt."

"Why?" another asked from the crowd.

"Because the more men that ride out will only cause more problems. It'll slow us down. It could alert the mayor, or anyone he may be working with, that we're on to them." He pointed behind him outside the gathered crowd. "I have Asher Walker with me. You all know him, know what he's capable of. Trust me to see this through."

One of the men stepped forward, the tendons in his neck straining beneath his skin. "We won't just sit here and wait. He can't get away with taking off with one of them."

"You're absolutely right. You can't just sit and wait." He looked over the crowd. "While I'm gone, the other women are left defenseless. Anyone could hurt or take them. If you all, as a group, station yourselves outside their house, warding off anyone in particular who gets any ideas from what the mayor has done, the rest will be safe. Can I count on you?" he asked the group.

It seemed to be the right thing to say to get them to back down. And it was the truth. If they were all intent on guarding the women, none of them would be able to go out there alone and take another. As a group, the men would wipe out anyone who dared.

"We'll take good care of them," the man said before turning to the crowd. "We have a job to do, men."

Sawyer watched them ride toward Ivan's house before he nodded to Asher. "Let's move."

They headed down the south road, looking for fresh tracks. There wasn't much need to ride to the next town on a daily basis, so he prayed it wouldn't be too difficult to spot clues.

If they couldn't, the only other hope was that Ronan had luck on the north road.

As time trickled by, both riding in silence, Sawyer couldn't help but think of the interaction between Asher and Ronan. There was a whole long, twisted history between the two of them that he didn't know enough about to diffuse. It was better for all that they'd separated. Not just for the ground they were able to cover, but because Sawyer worried having them in close proximity to each other would only distract Asher from tracking.

Sawyer didn't know the first thing about picking up a trail in the mountains. Weighing facts, examining crime scenes, that's where he excelled. But out here, out in the open, he was useless. He couldn't imagine Ronan was any better now that he thought of it. Going off on his own could actually make things worse.

Ronan was gifted in many ways, but he never traveled anywhere either. "Maybe we should've stayed together. I don't want to have to go after

Ronan when this is all over." Damn it, he was sick of worrying about everyone.

Asher's eyes never wavered from the trail. "He'll be fine. We trained together in the army. You don't need to worry about him getting lost or dying on the mountain."

The army?

That information both relieved and disturbed him. Sawyer would've never guessed that Ronan had been in the army. He was too calculating, too gun ready. But maybe that's where he learned those skills. War changed men.

If they were in the military together, wouldn't they be closer? The rift between the two men was so wide it seemed as if nothing could ever cross it. Something bad must've happened.

"There." Asher pointed out prints that splintered off the main road onto a lesser used trail. "It's fresh. They came this way. Or someone did. But this trail isn't normally used so I'd guess it was them."

Sawyer squinted up at the high sun, wondering if they'd catch them soon. They had to. He had to believe that. But the mayor had a good lead on them. The only thing in their favor was that Asher knew the mountains like he was born to them.

"Why this trail?" Sawyer asked. There wasn't anything around but wilderness. "It doesn't go anywhere."

"That's not true, exactly. It's an old road that eventually leads to the Montana Trail, but it's been abandoned since the road through Benton Pass made travel faster. I'd bet he's headed that way."

If he made it to the Montana Trail, he could stop

at any number of cities along the way and force Clara to marry him. "We have to find them before they reach it."

Asher's eyes hardened, deepening in color. "We'll get her before the bastard forces her to do anything."

Sawyer could only imagine how painful this must be for Asher. The one woman he'd loved had been kidnapped, but he hadn't found her in time to save her life.

This time, it'd be different. Sawyer staked his life on it.

CLARA STUMBLED THROUGH THE FOREST as spiky bushes pulled at her shredded skirts. Her arms ached from her bonds, and she'd lost all feeling in her hands long before.

If she could just get them free, she might have a chance to escape. As of now, she could neither fight nor run.

At least he'd loosened the gag. "Do you intend for me to walk the entire way to wherever we're headed?"

Bracken glared down at her. She refused to think of him as the mayor anymore. "The horse can't carry both of us. You're younger and stronger. You'll be fine walking."

It wasn't about who was younger or stronger. She was certainly capable of walking, but perhaps, if she could appeal to a gentlemanly side of him, she could get on the horse and escape. "I can't make it much farther with my hands tied. They're hurting and slowing us down. We could be a lot farther ahead if you'd loosen them. And my legs hurt." It took all her willpower to pout up at him with sad eyes when all she wanted to do was let fury fuel her muscles and lash out at him.

"Stop complaining. It's annoying. And I won't have an annoying wife."

Her blood went cold. "I will never be your wife."

He laughed then. "Yes you will. If you don't agree to marry me at the appropriate time, I'll make sure you pay for it. I'm sure the other women wouldn't take kindly to their only source of income being taken away. I can do that, you know. I gave it to them, and I can take it away."

Her feet planted in the ground. She didn't care if he continued on and dragged her body behind his horse. "If that's true, then why take me at all? You don't love me, and I certainly don't love you. Just take the mine."

His lips twisted. "How about Sheriff Morrison? Would you be so quick to disobey me if his life was on the line? It would be so unfortunate if he were to have an accident. Another cave-in, perhaps? Or a rogue bullet." He shrugged. "Those things happen."

She gasped. "You wouldn't."

"I would," he said flatly. "You don't want to test me."

"Why are you doing this? You don't want me."

He leaned back in his saddle. "Oh, but you're wrong there. I do want you, Clara. I want you very much."

"Why?"

"Because with you comes the mine. I want that gold. And by marrying you, it can never be taken from me."

Gold? All of this is over the fictional gold? Well the joke was on him. "I'm sorry to tell you, but there's no gold. We spread that lie to draw out the person sabotaging the mine… you. You've made the mistake. You get nothing by marrying me."

He laughed. "You're wrong there. Your lie might've sped up my decision to marry you, but it was going to happen anyway."

"Why?"

"Because there really is a mother lode. Ivan bragged to me about it the day before he died. Well, truth be told, the day before I killed him."

Her skin went clammy. "You killed Ivan?" She could barely get the words out. "How could you do such a thing?"

He shrugged. "I needed the gold. My mine never paid out. I kept looking, but it was barren. Ivan didn't need the gold. He didn't even care. All he wanted was that stupid house and his choice of bride. But would he sell? No. Last mistake he ever made. I poisoned him the next day."

Heavens. Bracken was a madman, and there'd be no reasoning with him. He wasn't driven by logic or conscience. Something darker drove him. Something infinitely more evil.

Something she could never escape from.

She glanced up at the waning sun. The others must know she was missing by now. They had to be searching for her.

But how would they find her? They'd been

wandering in the mountains for what seemed like days. Every passing tree looked the same. They could be going in circles for all she knew.

No one would come for her. It was up to her to save herself.

And when the opportunity presented itself, she'd fight.

She glanced at the gun resting across his lap.

If she didn't, she wouldn't survive.

As night came for the second time while being held captive, Clara was grateful that besides the mine, Bracken seemed to have no other designs on her.

"We'll reach the trail tomorrow and get another horse. We should arrive in the Idaho Territory soon if we can find one."

She could just imagine what finding one entailed. If he'd had the funds to purchase another mount, he would've done so long ago. The only question remained was if he would force her to steal one or if he would steal it himself.

She wouldn't wait to find out. If they made it to the Trail tomorrow, she'd have a harder time getting away. If she could escape into the forest, she might be able to find her way to the Trail, and from there, get help. But who would help her if she was with *Mayor* Bracken? She had a feeling, not many.

"I need to freshen up." It was the only time he released her hands, and she intended on making the most of it. She would've waited until he was sleeping, but as she'd learned last night, he didn't untie her even at night. In fact, he tied another rope around her wrists and tied it to his own.

"What the hell are you talking about now, woman?"

She rolled her eyes behind his back. So much for trying for delicacy. "Nature is calling."

If she was going to escape, it had to be now. There was no moon tonight, and it was dark. Dark enough that if she got a head start, she could get away from him.

He rose from the rock he was sitting on, grumbling at the inconvenience. Not that she'd had much need to relieve herself. Not with the pittance of water he'd allowed her.

Truth be told, the minute she was back home, she would glut herself on it. But first things first.

"Don't try anything stupid," he warned.

She bowed her head in a show of subservience, and she hoped it masked the flare of rage firing her eyes.

She would kill this man. If she ever got the chance, she would.

"Go on. Be quick about it."

She took a few steps into the trees. Then a few more when he didn't argue. He must feel confident that they were far enough away from civilization that she wouldn't try to escape. In his mind, he probably thought women couldn't survive alone in the wilderness.

She wouldn't argue with that. She wasn't sure she *could* survive. She'd never had to take care of herself in that way.

But if she had the choice between going at it alone or sticking with him, she would run toward the trees with as much speed as possible.

She squatted down, hands sifting through pine needles for a stick, branch, rock, or anything else she could use as a weapon.

Even though he'd allowed her the distance, she knew he listened to her every move. If she ran, she wouldn't get far. She had to hurt him. Take him down long enough to put some distance between them.

And then hide.

She closed her eyes in gratitude when her fingers closed around a thick branch. If she aimed right, hitting him in the head, this could do enough damage.

She rose slowly, kicking the needles around as if to cover a mess and hid the branch in her skirt folds. It was dark enough that she just might get away with it.

She walked slowly back to camp, hoping her steps sounded heavy and dejected. She didn't want him to realize what her plan was until it was too late.

But with every step she took closer to him, her pulse jumped and doubt crept in.

If she swung and missed, if she didn't hit him hard enough, he'd make her pay. She had to be sure, absolutely sure that she could do this, or she was signing her death warrant.

But what was the alternative? If she didn't do this, if she didn't try to escape, he would force her down the Trail to the next town with a preacher and marry her.

She would *not* be bound to this man. She'd rather die.

And she might.

"Come here," he ordered, and she dragged her feet over to him.

"Could you leave the bindings off? Just for tonight? I'd sleep better and have more energy for the trip tomorrow."

He spit. "Do as you're told, woman."

Her cheeks heated. He would never speak to her like that again.

She stepped forward, and the second he looked down at her hands, she lifted the branch and struck.

As she'd hoped, he hadn't expected it.

The impact to his head vibrated the branch all the way up her arm and forced the wood out of her hands.

But she didn't wait to see how much damage she'd done. When he went down, she ran.

Chapter Sixteen

When night fell, Sawyer was ready to tear off someone's head. Asher's was convenient. "We can't stop yet. We have to be close."

"If we keep going, one of our mounts will break a leg. It's too dark to continue."

Sawyer's fists clenched. "It's a chance I'm willing to take."

Sawyer tried to brush past him, but Asher held a hand to his chest. "I'm not. Not only will we injure the horses, but we can't see any tracks. We could miss something and be farther away from them when light hits. They would've stopped for the night. They aren't going anywhere tonight."

Asher waited until Sawyer nodded before dropping his hand. Understanding lit in the mountain man's eyes. Sawyer knew Asher had been here before, knew what he was going through. How could he remain so calm?

"Having a hot head will only put her in more

danger," Asher said, answering a question Sawyer hadn't realized he'd asked.

It made sense, but he couldn't just wait. He couldn't go to sleep when Clara could be injured, scared—or worse. Every fiber of his being screamed that he needed to find her, to keep her safe.

Until he held her once more, he'd find no rest, no peace.

Is this what love always felt like? He'd known the excitement and joy of loving Clara, but he hadn't realized that this constant fear of losing her could break him. He'd give anything to find her.

Asher tossed some jerky at Sawyer. "Try and get some rest."

Easier said than done. "Thank you for helping me."

Asher grunted, but didn't say more.

Sawyer didn't know the man well. Honestly, he hadn't even seen him more than a handful of times. He hadn't been around when Asher's woman was taken, but he'd heard the stories.

Everyone had.

The bastards that took her were never found, but Asher found her remains after she'd been mauled by a bear.

After that, he kept to himself in the mountains.

Sawyer felt bad for the guy, but a part of him, a part that he wasn't proud of, was grateful for the man's experience. Because if Asher hadn't lost his woman, he would've never secluded himself in the mountains. He would've never garnered the skills needed to find Clara—

A shot ran in the woods.

Sawyer jumped to his feet. "That was close."

Asher nodded, grabbing his gun before standing. "They're not far off."

Sawyer didn't care how much Asher argued. "I'm going after her."

"I'm coming with you."

Sawyer didn't need any more assurance. He ran into the trees, gun in hand as his arms and legs pumped in time with his breaths. "Clara!"

Another shot rang out, this time closer, and he went even faster, imagining the worst. "Clara!"

A scream filled the air.

❦

RUNNING BLINDLY THROUGH THE TREES, Clara didn't feel the tiny slices across her skin. She didn't look back at the crashing sounds behind her as Bracken closed in.

She hadn't hit him hard enough.

The first bullet grazed her right arm and planted in the tree next to her. But she didn't stop as pine needles hanging from branches lapped up the blood oozing from her wound.

"Get back here, you whore!"

She sucked in a breath of terror and almost screamed when another bullet flew past her.

She wasn't going to make it home.

He was going to kill her.

"Clara!"

She heard her name called but thought she was imagining it. When it was yelled a second time, she knew it was real. "Sawyer!"

Panic filled her. She wanted to run to him, to be safe once again, but that would lead Bracken to him.

She would never forgive herself, not in this life or the next, if something happened to him.

Her legs sagged from running. Breath burned in her lungs. And with one misstep, she tripped on a rock and crashed to the ground, screaming.

Pain blazed through her in waves until she saw stars.

She had to get up. She had to run.

She crawled a foot before a body slammed on top of hers.

She kicked and screamed, lashing out blindly as she fought off her kidnapper.

He smacked her, and a coppery taste filled her mouth. She moaned, flailing with waning energy.

"That was real stupid," he spat, easily holding her down. "Real stupid." He grabbed her by the hair and yanked her up. "You're going to pay for that."

She screamed as he pulled her along by her hair.

"Let her go."

Sawyer.

She closed her eyes. She wanted to cry with happiness now that he was here.

The mayor pulled her painfully tight in front of him, and a muffled cry escaped her lips when he squeezed her cut arm.

As the pain ebbed, she glanced around but couldn't see him.

"Stay back, Sheriff. If you want to keep the woman alive, I suggest you turn around and head back to town," the mayor called out to the trees, his head whipping around trying to find a target.

He cocked the gun behind her, and her eyes flew open. "He has a gun!"

He twisted her arm in retaliation.

Sawyer stepped from the trees, his gun aimed straight for them. "If you hurt her again, I'm going to shoot your brains out instead of arresting you."

Bracken ducked behind her, using her as a shield. "You'll have to shoot her before you get to me."

"True." Sawyer's head nodded behind them. "But he won't."

Before she could react, Bracken swung them around. A fierce, bearded man glared down at them with the lightest blue eyes she'd ever seen before hitting Bracken in the head with the butt of his rifle.

He collapsed to the ground like a felled deer, and two seconds later, Sawyer scooped her in his arms. "It's over. You're safe."

She tried to nod, but only succeeded in shivering. "Is he…"

"Dead?"

Still holding her tightly against him, he tucked her head into his chest and looked past her to the body on the ground. "No. He's alive."

She shuddered and wrapped her arms around him.

"I'll just give you two a minute," the other man said before dragging the mayor toward the trees.

Sawyer nodded his thanks before turning his full attention back to her. His hands ran up and down her body, both soothing and stimulating.

He made her feel safe and alive all in the same moment.

And she had almost lost that. Either one of them could've died. This could've ended so differently.

She sobbed into his chest, and he just held her, caressing her as she broke. "You're safe. You're all right. I'm here."

She held onto his words like an anchor during a storm. He was her compass, her map. He was everything to her.

Life was too short for anything but honesty. If something had happened to them, she would've never forgiven herself if she hadn't told him how she truly felt. "I love you, Sawyer." She arched away from him and met his eyes. "I love you."

His lips crushed down on hers, and she realized he'd been holding back. He'd been calm and soothing because that was what she'd needed. But now he needed.

She soothed him with her lips, with whispered words, and with tender hands, letting the storm of his emotions flood her, fill her. She wanted this, wanted him, wanted it all.

She kissed as wildly as he, lingering and deepening the connection with each sweeping pass.

He finally broke away from her, and his whole body shook as he gathered her close in his arms. "If anything ever happens to you—"

"It won't," she hurried to soothe. "I'll always be here."

He ripped her away from him, but kept his hands gentle. "Damn right you will. You're marrying me tomorrow and never leaving my side."

"All right," she said easily, her heart filling with joy.

"I mean it, Clara. We're getting married tomorrow," he said again, clearly not believing her.

"And I said all right."

The tension in his body slowly eased as his eyes softened. "You'll marry me?"

"It doesn't sound like I have much choice, does it?" she teased.

A laugh huffed from his chest. "You always have a choice. I love you. I want you to be my wife, but I'll never force it on you. No matter how much I need you. What you need comes first."

She cupped his cheek. "I need you. Just you, Sawyer."

And in the moonless night, her lips met his again.

She might have been alone when she'd come to Promise Creek, but she'd never be on her own again.

She'd found the other half of her heart.

Epilogue

Clara wiped the flour off her hands onto her apron. The pie she'd been cooking was one of Sawyer's favorites.

She glanced out the kitchen window of her recently built house and marveled at the view as she caressed her swelling belly. They'd picked out the land together shortly after they married, and she couldn't be happier. It was just outside of town, which allowed Sawyer to perform his duties as sheriff, but also provided them with some privacy. At least as much privacy as they could scrounge between visits from Ivan's eight other brides.

She rubbed her belly. "Your father will be home any minute. Do you think he'll like his surprise?"

She jumped when Sawyer's arms wove around her, his hands linking with hers over the baby. "I love any surprise from you."

He slowly turned her around.

Clara's eyes twinkled with moisture. It had to be

the babe. She was so much more emotional now that she was carrying a child.

Sawyer's finger traced the moisture, but didn't say anything. He had to be used to it by now, but he didn't complain. If anything, he loved her even more. And that love was quite a lot considering all he'd taken on with Ivan's mail-order brides since they'd married.

"You're beautiful," he said, placing a kiss on her lips.

She laughed through a sniff. "I'm huge."

"Beautiful," he stressed.

She didn't argue. She was too happy to do anything but relax in his arms.

Six months ago, they'd both been alone. Sure, she'd had the other women, and as far as she was concerned, she always would. All of Ivan's brides were bound together forever.

Even Violet. Clara snickered.

But that wasn't the same thing as having the other half of your soul. Sawyer and she were bound to each other. Now and forever.

Sawyer turned her in his arms with a questioning brow. "What is it?" he asked, always in tune with her.

"Just thinking about life. How it doesn't turn out how we think it will."

"And are you happy with the way things have turned out?"

He knew how much she loved him, but she reached out and soothed him anyway. "Blissful everyday."

His eyes narrowed playfully and she laughed. "I

mean it. I couldn't imagine my life any other way."

He brushed a kiss across her lips. "I love you."

"I love you too," she said, sighing into another kiss. Life couldn't get any better, indeed.

TITLES BY JANELLE DANIELS

ABOUT THE AUTHOR

JANELLE DANIELS is an award-winning and Amazon bestselling author.

Janelle wasn't one of those people who knew they were meant to write from a young age. After jumping from one hobby to the next, she discovered her passion for writing at nineteen. After one manic writing episode, Janelle was hooked.

A mother of two, Janelle spends her days chasing down the 'beasties' and her nights writing (poor husband). If she can spare a second after spending time with her family and writing, you can usually find her curled up to a computer, catching up on her latest TV show addiction.

TO SIGN UP FOR JANELLE'S NEW RELEASE NEWSLETTER, GO TO
www.JanelleDaniels.com

Janelle LOVES to hear from readers!

WEBSITE:
www.JanelleDaniels.com

FACEBOOK:
www.facebook.com/pages/Janelle-Daniels/155252004529054

TWITTER:
www.twitter.com/_JanelleDaniels

CPSIA information can be obtained
at www.ICGtesting.com
Printed in the USA
LVOW03s1734310118
564753LV00003B/710/P